"The night we met, I thought you had the most kissable mouth I had ever seen, and I wanted to kiss it right there and then," *Richard said.*

"I . . ." Sandy couldn't breathe. She stood there, feeling the heat of his body through her blouse, and felt herself swirling in the blue of his eyes.

"I thought about kissing you a lot during the past six weeks," he said huskily.

"H-have you?" Her hands sneaked out of her control and covered his where they lay on her waist. How hard his wrists were, how crisp the hair on them. He felt so different from the way she felt, the way her children felt. How long had it been since she'd touched someone who wasn't a child?

"And if you don't quit looking at me with those provocative big brown eyes, I'm going to do it right now," he warned.

She didn't stop, couldn't stop. She shivered as his bare legs touched hers below her shorts. This was a top-of-the-roller-coaster feeling, a holler-stop-before-it's-too-late feeling, but she could do no more than sigh as he brought his mouth to hers. . . .

WHAT ARE *LOVESWEPT* ROMANCES?

They are stories of true romance and touching emotion. We believe those two very important ingredients are constants in our highly sensual and very believable stories in the *LOVESWEPT* line. Our goal is to give you, the reader, stories of consistently high quality that may sometimes make you laugh, sometimes make you cry, but are always fresh and creative and contain many delightful surprises within their pages.

Most romance fans read an enormous number of books. Those they truly love, they keep. Others may be traded with friends and soon forgotten. We hope that each *LOVESWEPT* romance will be a treasure—a "keeper." We will always try to publish

*LOVE STORIES YOU'LL NEVER FORGET
BY AUTHORS YOU'LL ALWAYS REMEMBER*

The Editors

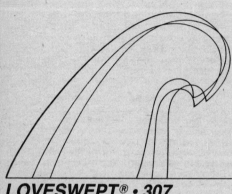

LOVESWEPT® · 307

Judy Gill
Light Another Candle

BANTAM BOOKS
TORONTO · NEW YORK · LONDON · SYDNEY · AUCKLAND

LIGHT ANOTHER CANDLE

A Bantam Book / February 1989

If you would be interested in receiving protective vinyl
covers for your Loveswept books, please write to this address
for information:

Loveswept
Bantam Books
P.O. Box 985
Hicksville, NY 11802

ISBN 0-553-21983-9

Published simultaneously in the United States and Canada

PRINTED IN THE UNITED STATES OF AMERICA

O   0 9 8 7 6 5 4 3 2 1

For
Nita Taublib,
who believed so strongly
and argued so staunchly,
proving that persistence pays.
Thanks.

One

Sandy Filmore parked her car and squinted in the bright sunlight that sliced through the clouds which, in typical Oregon fashion, were clearing now that day was nearly done. She glanced at her watch, gave a satisfied nod, and with quick fingers set the alarm on it. Tilting her seat back into a reclining position, she stretched out and in less than two minutes was asleep. Exactly thirty minutes later the warbling tone of her alarm woke her and she opened her eyes to discover that the sun had completed its descent behind the college administration building. Most of the clouds were gone, leaving a sunset-trimmed dome overhead that promised a beautiful tomorrow.

With another yawn, she sat up, checked her image briefly in the rearview mirror, smoothed her dark hair with both hands, and reached for her briefcase.

The opening car door connected solidly with a hard object, and she heard a muffled "Oof!" before it completed its swing. Startled, she jumped out to see a man lying facedown in a puddle left by the day's deluge.

"Oh, good heavens," she said. "Are you hurt? Let me help you."

He rose without her help and retrieved a dripping briefcase, held it out to let the water stream off, and glared at her.

"What happened?" she asked, reaching out to pluck a red and white gum wrapper from his sodden lapel.

"What happened?" he repeated. "You kicked me in the butt, that's what happened."

"I did not," she said indignantly, then recalled the thud as she had opened the car door. "I was just trying to get out of my car. How was I to know there was a weirdo skulking around below window level?" She backed up a step, wondering if he really was weird. He didn't look it, but one never knew. What had he been doing down there anyway?

As if reading her mind he said, "Stealing hubcaps. Letting air out of tires. Planting bombs. Take your pick."

Sandy continued to back away, never taking her eyes off him. He paced after her, still dripping, his white teeth flashing against the tan of his face. He was leering at her. That was the only word for it. His blue eyes glittered under a fall of thick, butter-colored hair that tumbled across his brow. As she rounded the rear of her car, he came abreast of the driver's door. He flicked a glance inside and then, sardonically, at her.

"What? No boyfriend? Usually when an occupied car looks empty, there's only one reason. Before I bent down to tie my shoe I didn't see anyone in there."

"I could have been changing fuses," she snapped. "But the truth is, I was sleeping."

"At seven in the evening?"

"It's seven-thirty," she said as if there were some justification in those extra minutes. "And working mothers have to sleep when and where they can." If he knew she was a mother, would he leave her alone? "You'll have to excuse me. I have a class."

"Not until you give me your name and address."

Her brown eyes widened. "Get lost!"

"Nope." He smiled—leered, actually—and her heart rate increased. "I need to know where to send the cleaning bill," he added.

Cleaning bill? Good heavens, was that disappointment she felt? He wanted her address only to send her a cleaning bill for something that had been his own fault entirely?

Her attempted laugh came out all jangled and tinny. "Forget that, mister. Now, get away and leave me alone." Her voice rattled with incipient panic as he stepped even nearer, and she felt herself come up against the side of a big van that effectively hid her and the man from the sight of people using the main entrance of the college.

"Get away from me. I'm warning you, just leave me alone," she repeated, her jaw squared. She snapped open her gray leather shoulder bag and reached a hand inside hoping he'd think she had a dangerous dagger, a police whistle, a can of Mace. . . .

He laughed then, and the warm, comforting sound of it startled her. Could a weirdo have such a nice laugh?

"Hey, come on," he said gently, sounding not at all weird. "I'm not going to hurt you. And I would like to get to know—" He broke off as, to Sandy's weak-kneed relief, a booming voice rang out. "Dr. Gearing! So there you are. I was beginning to think you'd been de—oh, I see, you've met our Miss Filmore." The dean of education added that last as if it explained everything.

Sandy let out her breath in a whoosh when the stranger's eyes looked laughingly into hers.

"Good evening, Dr. French," he said, extending a slightly damp hand toward the dean. "Miss Filmore and I hadn't quite got to the point of exchanging names. Perhaps you would do the honors? I'm afraid she has the impression I'm not altogether trustworthy."

"Hmmph!" snorted the dean, casting a chiding glance at Sandy. She bristled, ready to defend herself, but he sighed and added, "Well, well, I suppose a young woman can't be blamed for being wary of a stranger in a parking lot." He bestowed a forgiving smile on her and said, "Sandra Filmore, meet Dr. Richard Gearing, whom I hope we'll convince to join us as head of the marketing faculty. Sandra is a member of our extended education program. She's giving a series of lectures on landscaping."

"Rick," he said as his hand engulfed hers in a warm clasp that tingled all the way up her arm.

"Sandy," she said, and found her gaze captured by his. His fingers moved over the skin of her hand as if he liked the feel of it. She felt her stomach flutter crazily, and, to her horror, felt her nipples respond to the sensation of his fingers on her hand just as if they had touched her breast. Startled, she jerked her hand from his clasp and stepped back from him, her eyes wide.

His looked startled, too, and she was weakened by the sudden conviction that he had shared her wild reaction to their skin's contact. She was grateful when Dr. French urged him toward the entrance.

Sandy followed several paces behind the men, not hearing their conversation, but acutely aware of the rich timbre of Rick Gearing's voice, its resonance deep and smoky. She watched his long legs as he ascended the steps, saw the play of muscles in his thighs as his pants tightened with his smooth, easy strides. He moved with the unconscious grace of a man in superb physical condition. What kind of daily workout did he prefer, she wondered, and was immediately surprised at herself for wondering. She was normally much too busy to spend any idle moments thinking about men.

She thought she'd been forgotten until she entered the building and found him waiting for her. "What time is your—"

"My word, man," Dr. French interrupted. "What happened to you?"

"Nothing serious," Rick replied. "I had a small accident in the parking lot. One of your minor lakes reached up and attacked me. I hope there's a place I can repair some of the damage before I meet the board."

"Of course, of course. Right this way," said Dr. French, taking his arm, clearly having forgotten Sandy again, which wasn't surprising and was fine with her. Part-time staff members ordinarily didn't hobnob with the college elite. The reason the dean even remembered her name, she was sure, was that her twin daughters always attracted attention, but never more so than when one of them had spilled cranberry cocktail all over him at the Christmas party.

Richard Gearing deftly removed his arm from the older man's clasp and reached out to capture Sandy's elbow as she started to walk away. His hand slid down her sleeve until their fingers were joined, and again she felt that tingling sensation. "I don't suppose my meeting with the board will take long. After your class may I buy you a drink to thank you for . . . helping me when I fell?"

Sandy hesitated, torn between the desire to explore the reason behind the sensation he aroused in her and an instinct for self-preservation that was hollering "Watch out!"

"Please?" he asked softly. "As a favor? To . . . cancel any other debts?" A gentle reminder, she thought, of the cleaning bill he had mentioned.

She had to smile. "What one person might consider reason for indebtedness, another might not, Dr. Gearing. If you were to buy me a drink, then I *might* feel under an obligation."

"Ah, but then you could buy me one, and we'd be even."

"I never have more than one," she said with reluctance.

"You can reciprocate when I come back." He smiled. "When I join the faculty here."

Something very similar to the excitement she had infrequently felt as a teenager now fluttered through her even though she was ten years past her teens. She returned his smile. "That being a foregone conclusion?" she asked.

"It is now," he said, "if the board wants me." And suddenly neither of them was smiling. Dr. French and his impatiently tapping toe were only a dimly perceived intrusion on a very private moment.

Sandy drew in a deep breath that somehow failed to provide the oxygen she required. "Room

315, nine-thirty," she said, realizing that if they stood there any longer lost in each other's eyes, his chance of becoming a member of the faculty might very well be diminishing with every impatient breath Dr. French drew.

She slid her hand from the warmth of his and turned to walk away, sensing his intent gaze on the sway of her hips and the swing of the pleated skirt of her green suit as it flirted against the backs of her knees. She was glad she had worn her highest heels, the ones that made her legs look great. It made her aware of her femininity. And suddenly she realized that it had been a long, long time since she had felt good about herself as a woman.

The nine-thirty date was a bust. She should have known better than to suggest the bar frequented by the faculty and students. Even though she'd never been there, she should have realized it wasn't the spot for a getting-to-know-you conversation. The place was humming and the quiet corner table they'd asked for couldn't have stayed quiet for more than fifteen minutes, Sandy thought. She hardly cared what they talked about; all that seemed important was the sound of his voice and the warmth and appreciation in his gaze.

She told him about how she'd come to love Portland in the six months she'd lived there; how, even in winter the multitude of parks and public gardens were worth visiting.

He told her about the high-pressure business of market consulting in New York, and how he had just sold his share of a partnership in such a company and was now searching for a less stressful environment. He hoped to find it in Portland.

She hoped he would find it in Portland.

But as the bar filled up, her opportunity to find out why he wanted to make such a change disappeared. The extra chairs at their table were occupied and the sounds of conversation and laughter drowned their heart-to-heart talk. People demanded introductions to the possible new head of marketing. If Rick had made a firm decision as a result of his meeting with the board, or if the board had, he kept the information to himself. Wishing again and again that she'd chosen a different place, Sandy finally stood, excused herself by saying that she couldn't keep her teenage babysitter up any longer on a school night.

He stood with her and walked her to her car. There, he took her hand again and held it loosely. In the dark she was unable to read his expression, even though she knew his eyes were on her face.

"Not quite what I had in mind when I asked you for a drink," he said softly.

"I'm sorry." She withdrew her hand and got into her car. "Good-bye, Rick."

Holding the door so she couldn't close it, he

smiled at her and said, "Make that good night. Happy dreams, Sandy. Sleep well." Then, before she could respond, he closed the door of her car and turned, striding back toward the noisy tavern.

Sandy stared after him for a long time before beginning the drive home.

Her common sense had returned by the time she pulled into the driveway, arched over with grapevines. What had gone on between her and Richard Gearing had been nothing more than a mild flirtation, and by the time he would arrive to start the summer session at the college, if indeed he did so, her course would be finished and she would no longer be there. If all went well with her fledgling landscaping business and the nursery she had inherited from her grandmother, there would be no need for her to take a teaching job again in the fall and she would have no occasion to see him. Fortunately, now that she was no longer exposed to the magnetism of his incredibly blue eyes, she could see the attraction they had both experienced for what it had been—a fleeting, nebulous thing, not to be repeated because she, for one, had much too busy a life to get involved with a man. She congratulated herself on achieving this insight a month later, when she learned that Richard Gearing had a child.

It had been a bit of a shock to hear Dr. French's secretary asking another woman if she knew of any good private preschools, because a new faculty member, one Richard Gearing, needed that for his four-year-old son. The shock had been not that he had a son, but that he was coming at all. So much time had passed that she had convinced herself he had changed his mind, or the board had decided against him. It was also a shock to discover some small thing deep inside herself leaping and dancing with excitement she was totally unable to suppress, in spite of the severe and frequent lectures she gave herself.

Two weeks later her series of lectures was finished, and Rick Gearing, if he had arrived, had made no attempt to contact her. She told herself she was not disappointed, and even managed to persuade herself that not only did the man have a child, in every likelihood he also had a wife, and that was why he hadn't been in touch. No, she had been right in the beginning; it had been nothing more than a mild flirtation, and the sooner she forgot about it, the better. She had a business to run and two children to raise and no room in her days or evenings for any kind of romantic relationship.

Her nights, however, she couldn't control. At least not the dreams that filled them.

But during the day she checked invoices from suppliers and issued statements to customers. She tried to write the same compelling advertising copy her late grandmother had apparently been capable of and failed, because all she wanted to do was design and plant. She found herself sneaking away from office duties too often, sketchbook in hand, to find another freshly cleared lot that she could landscape if only in imagination.

Again unable to concentrate, she set aside the still-unfinished payroll, and indulged in memories of the day she and her twin daughters, Jenny and Pam, had arrived, half apprehensive, half excited. It was the first time they'd seen the property left to Sandy by the grandmother she'd never known.

It had been raining that October afternoon. . . .

AABAB NURSERY GARDENS the sign read, and, turning, she drove through a thirty-foot tunnel of greenery from which hung clusters of grapes, fat and purple and smoky. Then, as the car emerged from the archway, the sun came out as if on cue, bathing the scene with golden light, and Sandy was filed with an uncanny sense of homecoming.

She stopped the car and sat staring for a long time at the confusion of color and shape and size and texture that was spread before her. Dahlias grew in great profusion, in multitudes of colors. In a pond swam fat, lazy ducks nibbling at floating greenery. A stream bubbled between more clumps of asters, under a humpy-back bridge and chuckled away out the lower edge of the pond to disappear behind a massive fuchsia bush, still in full bloom.

Sandy heard herself laughing with abandon, all apprehension gone. Drawn to the edge of the water, she stood breathing in the pungency of the flowers. " '*Asters by the brookside make asters in the brook . . .*' " she quoted, and then whirled, startled, when a voice spoke behind her.

"That's what *she* always said, Sandra. Guess that's why she planted them there."

"Clara Aabab? My grandmother?"

The old man nodded. He was a little gnomelike creature with pale blue eyes and a fringe of white hair on a pink scalp. His smile was tentative until Pamela appeared, running across the bridge toward her mother. At the sight of the little girl he beamed.

"Mom," said Pam, her voice half strangled with excitement. "Come and see what we found. Please!" Her sister, impetuous, impatient, not content merely to ask, leapt the stream, disdaining the bridge, and tore to Sandy's side.

She skidded to a halt, looked up at the old man, and smiled winningly. "Hi," she said. "I'm Jenny. Are you Abe?"

The old man looked from one child to the other, grinned more broadly, and scratched his head. "Yup," he said. "Welcome home."

Sandy wondered at the glint of tears she thought she saw in Abe's eyes, but Jenny was tugging on her hand, rushing on. "Mom! You gotta *see*! There's two little houses over there! They've got our names on them! Mine and Pammy's!"

With the old man close behind, Sandy followed the girls over the bridge and past a stand of rhododendrons taller than her head to a grassy area where, sure enough, there were two little houses, just the right size for the girls, and they did have their names carved in the lintels over the doors. Sandy bent and peered into one. Pamela, sitting on a three-legged stool beside a small wooden table, grinned out at her, all golden and curly and glad.

Sandy turned to the old man and said, "Who built them? When?"

"I did. Soon's we learned you had twin baby girls. She always hoped you'd bring them to visit us someday."

Sandy stepped back from the silent accusation in his eyes. "But I didn't even know I had a grandmother," she defended herself. "Not until I got a letter from her lawyer saying she had died and left me this place."

"Oh, that boy," lamented the old man. "How much damage he did with his hate."

"Who?"

"Your father. He couldn't forgive. So he hid his past from his present and his future, and he died still hating his mother and me."

Sandy sensed Abe's sadness and impulsively hugged him. There had been more to his relationship with her grandmother than simply nursery business, and she recognized that not only had she found a home in Abe, but also, perhaps, a family.

After a moment of startled embarrassment he hugged her back. Together, they stood there with the sound of the children's laughter rising and falling around them, and the gurgle of the stream forming a background.

"It's good that you're here," said Abe at last. "*She's* glad too."

Now Sandy looked up from the payroll book she had been ignoring for much too long. The girls were in school, so there was no sound of children's laughter. It was quiet, too quiet, and then she realized with a surge of anger that she couldn't hear the gurgle of the stream that ran through the place from top to bottom.

She grabbed a key and marched out of the office, listening intently for the sound she should have been able to hear. It was not her imagination. The sound was absent. "He's dammed it!" she muttered furiously, swinging away up the path that followed the bed of the stream.

"Damn, damn, damn," said a cheerful but raucous voice overhead, and a heavy black body dropped straight down to land on her shoulder.

"Oh, Never," said Sandy in despair. "How am I going to get you to clean up your act? I wasn't cussing, much as I feel like it." He clung to her shoulder as she stormed on up the hill and she continued to address him. "Stick with me, friend. If I have to take on that lousy developer again, I might need you to peck him on the top of his bald head. Can't the man understand a simple court order?"

She unlocked the gate and went through the opening in the ten-foot-high chain-link fence that separated her property from the subdivision road beyond.

She scrambled up the bank and across the road to the driveway of the new glass-and-cedar house that the developer was certain would never sell at any price with a waterfall tumbling noisily right outside the master bedroom. And there, at the back of the house, where the stream should have been cascading down the fifteen-foot rock face, there was only a thin, muddy trickle, just as it had been when the developer dammed and diverted the flow last December. As she flung herself at the rock face, the raven deserted her, flying to the branches of a nearby cedar tree.

Sandy climbed swiftly from foothold to foothold, gaining one muddy knee, one wet foot, and the top of the cliff, where she discovered that the blockage was a natural one, created by Mother Nature sweeping her forest clean. Still, it had to be removed.

Working carefully so as not to fill the stream with rubble she'd have to scoop out of her own pond and pools, she began tugging at the branches and rocks that formed the dam. When, with a sudden and exuberant rush, the water broke free, she jumped back. The spouting of water elicited an outraged shout from somewhere below.

At the edge she saw a wall of water breaking over the head and shoulders of a man who had been climbing up as she had. The force sent him staggering backward, bouncing from ledge to ledge toward the now rapidly filling pool at the foot of the waterfall. Arms windmilling, he was borne backward and disappeared.

Somehow, she was down the cliff and into the pool in moments, her arms sweeping through the murky water until one hand caught in his hair. She tightened her grip and towed him to the side, lifting his head while he gagged and spewed out water.

"Dammit," he said, coughing as he got to his feet, "will you let go of my hair?"

Sandy did and stood staring at him through the curtain of water streaming from her own hair. She squeezed her eyes shut and then opened them again. Yes. It was still he. And for the second time, she had soaked him, but now to the skin.

In a voice that couldn't conceal a bubble of laughter, a hint of breathless joy, she said, "Oh! Hi. I thought you weren't coming."

Two

"You didn't think I was coming?" he said, reaching out to brush the hair off her face. In spite of his cold dunking, his hand was warm. "And if you had, what kind of reception would you have prepared? Target practice with a water bomber? Dare I ask why you were playing in my creek, Sandra Filmore?"

"Yours?" she asked faintly, feeling panic sweep over her to mingle with undeniable excitement. Where was all her common sense? What had happened to her resolve not to think about this man? Gone! Washed away by the waters of the stream, diluted to the point of no return by the power of his laughing blue eyes.

"Mine," he said firmly, cupping a hand around the back of her neck—and she recognized with a tinge of hysteria that he wasn't still talking about the stream; his eyes told her that the word had been applied directly to her. She shivered and stepped away from him.

"That stream happens to be mine, farther down," she told him. "I thought the developer had dammed it again, but it was a natural blockage."

"So, not having him to punish, you decided to take your anger out on me?" He grinned as he took off his light gray windbreaker and wrung it out.

Sandy swallowed, unable to look away from the broad expanse of his chest, where cold-shriveled nipples stood out, dark and clearly defined under his wet T-shirt.

"I . . . I didn't know you were there," she said, hurriedly snapping her attention back to his face. "You must have heard me splashing. Why didn't you say something?"

"I didn't hear a thing." He draped his jacket over a shrub, lifted one foot, and took off a loafer, spilling the water out. Then, setting the shoe down, he peeled off a muddy white sock, squeezing it hard with strong fingers. "The real estate guy warned me about the irritable woman who lives downstream and has fits if anything happens to her creek. Seeing it blocked, I figured I'd better find out why, and fix it. Fast."

Sandy only gaped at him. Having finished wringing out his socks, Richard Gearing was calmly unzipping his jeans. He skinned them down his lean, tanned thighs. His legs were covered by golden, curling hairs. He had good knees and well-shaped calves. She concentrated on them in order not to look at his wet black briefs.

"Enjoying yourself?" he asked, sounding smug.

"Oh!" Sandy gasped, her eyes darting back to his face. It was obvious that he was enjoying himself. She spun away from him. What was he doing? Even more to the point, what was she doing staring at him like some sex-starved maniac?

"Thank you!" said a raucous voice. Then, again, "Thank you, thank you!" Sandy twisted around to find Rick zipping up the jeans he had mercifully put back on. He was staring up at the cedar branches overhead.

"Are you a ventriloquist?" he asked, swinging his gaze down to her stricken face.

"Oh, no! Never!" She nearly moaned, not answering his question as a sickening sense of doom swept over her. She knew who had spoken and knew exactly what kind of offering would elicit such effusive thanks. "Did you leave something small and shiny lying around?" she asked over her shoulder, already in motion, lunging across the creek even as he replied, "Just my car keys on the railing of the deck."

She groaned as she ran, hoping desperately that the dratted bird would still be standing around admiring the keys, that by some miracle it would not be too late to rescue them, that she could reach the rail of the deck before Never escaped. What a dream! What a futile hope! She was too late, of course.

With a flash of glistening black wings the raven took off to a high branch. "Never, you bring those back! Dammit, get down here!" she shouted, hands on hips, a toss of her head flipping her hair back out of her eyes again.

"That," said Rick, "is one hell of a big mynah bird."

"That," retorted Sandy, still glaring up toward the treetops, "is a raven, and he's going to be *soup* if he doesn't get back down here. Right this minute, Never!"

"A raven? A talking raven? What is he, your familiar?"

"No. And he doesn't belong to me. He lived with my grandmother." At this point she was certainly not going to admit ownership. Especially since she didn't own Never. No one did. Never owned the people he favored with his presence. Or so Never seemed to think.

"And he has a thing about keys?"

"Keys above all, maybe because they rattle, but he likes almost anything small and shiny. My grandmother taught him to say thank you by giving him dimes."

Shading her eyes, she decided to try a different tactic. "Never, come on, sweetie. Come and see what Sandy has." Trouble was, Sandy had nothing, and Never knew it. He cut loose with the rest of his repertoire, none of it repeatable.

"Wow!" Rick was impressed. "What did your grandmother use to teach him that, silver dollars?"

"No. I mean, she didn't teach him that. He came to her already knowing those words. She tried to get him to clean up his act, but with as little success as I've had." She sighed and looked at the dark blue Buick in the driveway. "I suppose your car is locked and you don't have a spare set of keys?" What did locksmiths charge for house calls, assuming they even made them? Whatever it was, it would be more than she could afford, darn it.

"My car is locked," he said, grinning, "and I do have a spare set of keys."

"Wonderful." Sandy relaxed.

"Only one thing. The spare keys are in a suitcase in the trunk, along with the dry clothes I'd sure like to have."

They both watched as Never left his treetop and sailed for home. Although she willed it as strongly as she could, Sandy didn't see any glittering silver keys fall from his beak as he flew.

She sighed again and turned to look up at Rick. What was she going to do with him?

"Now what?" he said. "I stand here and drip dry?" He slid one hand around her arm and let it trail down until their fingers were linked, then he smiled a slow, potent smile that made her toes curl up inside her wet sneakers. He reached out and took her other hand, gently gripping her fingers. "On second thought," he said softly, "let's just stay close like this, and I'll steam dry instead."

Quickly, she pulled her hands from his while trying to look repressive, a difficult task when, she was sure, her own clothing had to be sending up wisps of steam.

"You'd better come down to my place. I can give you something to wear while I wash and dry your clothes. By then, Never will have gotten tired of your keys."

But, she wondered as they walked down the path beside the creek, when Never tired of playing with the keys, where was he likely to leave them? She could only hope it was somewhere in plain sight.

"Be careful, the grass is—

"—slippery here," she finished breathlessly, her warning having come too late as his feet shot out from under him and he cannoned into her. He landed on his back and she landed on her front— on top of his front. She stared into bright blue eyes only inches from her own, felt the hard length of him beneath her, felt the sizzle of their contact with each breath she took.

"Yes, indeed," he said, his eyes full of mirth. "The grass is slippery here. It's nice grass you grow, Sandy. You could patent it."

She squelched what could have come out only

as an inane, girlish giggle. And since she was neither inane nor girlish, she was appalled by the responses Rick inspired in her. "Um . . . would you be good enough to take your hands off my bottom?"

For an instant his fingers tightened. "Must I?"

"You must."

"You insist?"

"I do."

He nodded after a moment's consideration. "Okay," he said, and then slid his hands from her buttocks to the tops of her thighs.

Sandy's eyes widened. "*Doctor* Gearing!"

"Ms. Filmore," he mocked her.

She couldn't help it. She laughed, and instead of the inane giggle she had feared, the sound was husky and sultry and totally alien to her nature. "Let me go, you idiot!" She had to regain control of herself.

"I'd be an idiot if I did, but my mother's always telling me I lack sense when it comes to women. However, first this . . ."

He captured the back of her head with one hand, drawing her face down to his as his lips touched hers almost tentatively, then, as hers parted in surprise, he took them with a sureness that left her weak and breathless after only a moment.

The response of her body dismayed her with its white-hot flare of desire, and she wrenched herself free, shooting to her feet before he could hold her back.

"I thought it would be like that," he said quietly, getting to his feet. "Somehow, I was sure it would. Were you?"

For a moment she didn't answer. She thought of pretending she didn't know what he was talking about, thought of lying, of shrugging it all off. She knew, though, after one sidelong glance at him, the futility of equivocation.

"I was afraid it would be," she said.

"Afraid?" He frowned. "Why be afraid of a perfectly normal reaction between two unattached adults of opposite sexes?" Taking her shoulder in a surprisingly rough gesture, he spun her around. "You're not married, are you?"

"I . . . no. No, of course not."

"Good." There was satisfaction in his tone. "I didn't really think you were."

"Why not?"

"The way you responded to that kiss. No woman who was being regularly loved by the man she loved would have kissed back like that."

She glanced at him over her shoulder and began to walk on. "You sound pretty smug, Dr. Gearing," she said. "Maybe I'm just promiscuous."

He laughed and fell into step beside her. "Now, that," he said, "might bear investigation."

"Smug again," she snapped.

"I guess so," he said contritely. "Sorry. I'll try not to do it again if you'll promise not to call me Doctor. I never use the title."

"Okay, Rick."

They walked in silence for a few minutes, passing through a plantation of small apple trees whose pink blossoms made pale mist against the green grass.

"Anyway," he said, "you told me six weeks ago that single mothers sleep when and where they can. Are you divorced?"

"Yes. And I'm sure I must have said 'working' mothers."

"How many kids do you have? What are they? How old?"

"Girls. Twins. Eight."

He came to a halt and stared at her. "Eight sets of twin girls?"

Sandy laughed, amused by the vision of herself surrounded by sixteen Pams and Jennys. "No. One set of twins, aged eight. Jennifer and Pamela."

"It's hard raising kids alone, isn't it? Does their father help?"

"No," she said shortly. She didn't want to discuss her situation. "Are you divorced? I heard someone at the college mention that you have a son."

"Yes. Roger's four. I just got custody. He's the major reason I had for leaving New York. His mother lives there."

Sandy frowned up at him as they both came to a halt near one of the pools. "Excuse me, but are you deliberately trying to make it hard for his mother to see him?"

"Not at all." Suddenly, his expression was forbidding. "I'm only trying to make it easier for him to adjust. He's staying with my mother for a while until I get settled."

"But his mother? I mean, I identify with her and I think . . . I think it would be terrible if you kept her son away from her."

"There are things in life more terrible," he said, but didn't elaborate. After a brief pause he took her arm and walked on. "Having just gotten sole custody of a four-year-old, I don't know the first thing about the problems I'll be facing, except that there will be problems. It would be nice to be able to count on the help of a neighbor—and friend—who has some experience."

Sandy hesitated. Something in his darkened eyes appealed for understanding, but she couldn't think of anything more awful than being deprived of her children and it was still hard to accept that he moved so far away from his ex-wife. Of course, there could be extenuating circumstances. Only what? What could any woman do that was so heinous she had to be deprived of her child? She knew there were things, naturally, but surely a man as nice as Rick Gearing wouldn't have married a monster in the first place. Oh, she didn't know. But she did know about being a single parent.

"I'll help if I can," she promised. "But let's walk faster. You're shivering."

As they walked up the steps to the back porch, she gave him a twinkling smile and said, "This is another member of my family. Her name is Gloria. My grandmother planted her for me the day I was born." She stroked the leaves of a tiny, twisted oak tree in a pot.

According to Abe, Clara Aabab had said, "That will be for her. I'll grow it just for her, look after it, tend it as I would like to tend her, and sometime, maybe, she'll come to visit and I can give it to her."

That first day, with Clara no longer there to make the presentation herself, Abe had done it in her stead, as solemnly and as formally as if he were investing her with an order. In the same spirit she had accepted it, and as her grandmother had, she now tended it carefully.

It was almost eerie, she had thought since then, that bonsai had long been an interest of hers— almost as if she had known about Gloria.

"You might find the house a little . . . different," she said as she opened the back door. "The girls and I thought it was downright bizarre, but we left it pretty much as we found it. It grew on us. You see, I never knew the grandmother who left it to me, so I felt that keeping her things the way she'd had them might help me come to know her in some way or other."

She didn't add that she'd been unable to wipe away all of Abe's memories in a redecorating blitz, or that she was completely unable to afford to do it either.

As she opened the back door, she added, "The dirty dishes, however, are all mine."

Rick gaped. "It looks like a cross between a kindergarten classroom and a trivia museum." His laugh held only amazement and delight.

Sandy echoed it, amused by his reaction to seven hundred and fourteen—she and the girls had counted—picture postcards adorning the walls, interspersed with commemorative plaques and plates and cups and saucers from every great occasion back to, and including, the Chicago World's Fair. There were dozens of Christmas and Easter and Mother's Day cards, most of them handmade and most from children. It had been immediately clear to Sandy that her grandmother had been a much-loved member of the community.

"Wait till you see the living room. But first, into the shower with you."

"What about you? You're cold and wet too."

His twinkling eyes seemed to suggest that she could share. She ignored the invitation. "I'll use the one in the decontamination shed."

"Decontamination?" His blue eyes narrowed suspiciously.

"Sometimes we have to use pesticides. I'll bring you something to wear and put those things through the laundry. In there." Gently she shoved him toward the bathroom.

When she returned, the door was ajar. She thrust her arm through the opening. "I think this should fit."

She felt the heavy navy and white velour robe rise from her hand. "Obviously," he said, "this doesn't fit you. Are you hiding a live-in boyfriend from me, Sandy?"

"Not at all, and if I have one, why should I hide him? I'm twenty-nine years old and free to do whatever I want. However, that was a Christmas present for my husband. Only he didn't hang around long enough for Christmas that year." She thought of how she'd saved for it, too, hoping against hope that for once they would have a pleasant, truly peaceful Christmas. In fact, without Alex, she and the girls had had just that.

There was a moment's silence, then, "And you've kept it hoping he'd come back? For how long?"

She laughed. "I've kept it for three years as sort of an insurance policy. You know, like keeping baby clothes?"

"I don't know. And I don't see the insurance value of either," he said through the door.

Sandy laughed again. "No? You didn't know that the minute a woman gives away the last article of baby clothing she's sure to get pregnant again?"

He hooted derisively. "That's some kind of birth control! No wonder there are so many unwanted babies running around."

"Don't scoff. Look at me, for instance. I've kept two little pairs of sleepers and one man-sized bathrobe. No more babies. No more husband."

"And that's the way you want it?" came Rick's soft question.

That was the way it had to be! Sandy drew in a deep breath. "That's the way I want it."

The sound of the shower precluded any further conversation, and she went into the bathroom to collect Rick's wet things.

She was back in the house, showered and dressed and in her bedroom brushing out her long hair when his shower finally stopped. She put on a bit of makeup, sprayed a touch of perfume behind her ears, and then frowned at her reflection. "What are you doing, dummy?"

She noticed how bright her brown eyes looked, how full of life and happiness and . . . eagerness. "Oh, what the hell," she muttered. "What's wrong with wanting to look nice for a change?"

"Nice is the wrong word." Rick appeared in the mirror, and she whirled around to face him. "Even soaking wet with your hair all over your face you look beautiful, Sandy."

She wanted to tell him not to be ridiculous. She knew she wasn't beautiful. She wasn't even close to it. But something in his eyes held back her argument. Something in his eyes made her feel, for the first time in her life, that maybe, in some ways, she *was* beautiful. It was a strange and heady feeling, one she knew she must not get used to.

"How do I look?" he asked, spreading his arms wide, the sleeves of the robe sliding back to reveal muscular forearms liberally covered with the same golden hair she could see between the lapels.

"Fine," she said, hoping to sound blasé, but sounding, instead, much like Never.

"And so do you. Green suits you. You were wearing green the first time I saw you."

"Was I? I don't remember."

His mocking look told her he knew she lied. She crowded around him to get out of the small room, and he followed her into the laundry room.

"I have to turn on the washer. I couldn't do it with you in the shower or I'd have scalded you. Or frozen you. Depending on the setting. I always forget to check. Ruin more sweaters that way . . ." Her voice trailed off as she realized she was babbling. She gathered up the wet laundry, his and hers, light and dark, and crammed it, willy-nilly, into the machine. Rick reached around her and changed the setting. She gasped for breath. He was using up all the oxygen in the room.

"It was set on hot," he said, "so it would have been fine. I could have done with a cold shower." He smiled at her, lowered his voice, and added, "I still could. You have that effect on me."

A weak "Oh," was all she seemed capable of. Slowly, he lifted his hands, and placed them on her waist.

"You had that effect on me that first night, you know. I thought then that you had the most kissable mouth I had ever seen and I wanted very badly to kiss it right there and then."

"I . . ." She had to swallow. She bit her lower lip. She should have shoved him away and she knew it, but it was as if all her strength were going into the task of preventing her knees from collapsing. She could only stand there, feeling his heat through her blouse, feeling herself swirling into the blue of his eyes, losing ground with every second.

"I thought a lot about kissing you during the past month and a half," he said huskily.

"H-have you?" Her hands sneaked out of her control and covered his where they lay on her waist. How hard his wrists were. How crisp the hair on them. He felt so very different from the way she felt, the way her children felt. How long was it since she had touched someone who wasn't a child?

"And if you don't quit looking at me with those big, provocative brown eyes, I'm going to do it right now," he warned softly.

She didn't stop, couldn't stop. She shivered as his bare legs touched hers below her shorts. She needed to breathe, but had no strength to pull in air. This was a top-of-the-roller-coaster feeling, a holler-stop-before-it's-too-late feeling, but she had no breath to do more than sigh softly as she tilted her face to his.

His mouth, gentle at first, hardened as if he couldn't prevent it. His kiss was warm and cool at the same time . . . until it gradually heated and he explored her mouth with his tongue slowly, no hurry about him, no urgency, only soul-pervading sweetness that left her clinging helplessly to him.

"Wonderful," he said on a long breath, sliding his mouth to the lower edge of her right ear. "What a beautiful beginning."

Sandy felt the weight of his chest against her breasts as she leaned back against the washer and slowly remembered where she was.

"This is crazy, necking in the laundry room like a couple of teenagers."

"I for one never necked in a laundry room when I was a teenager," he said "Did you have some more comfortable place in mind?"

"I did not." She pushed him away. "And for that matter, I didn't neck in a laundry room either."

"No?" Her shove had moved him only a few inches away. "Where did you do your necking when you were a teenager, Sandy?"

"I didn't," she said flatly, and sailed past him. "And I think it's time I offered you some coffee."

"Try offering me some breakfast," he said, following her out of the room. "I drove all night and didn't stop once to eat."

"What in the world did you do that for?" She had driven all the way from Ohio last year and six hours behind the wheel had been about all she could take.

"The memory of a brown-eyed lady with midnight hair kept drawing me onward," he said lightly, entering the kitchen right behind her.

She flashed him a skeptical look over her shoulder as she filled the coffeemaker.

"That's the truth!" he protested her obvious disbelief.

"Hmmph," she said. "Bacon and eggs?"

Three

They had just finished eating when the intercom buzzed. Sandy reached over and thumbed down the button. "I'm here," she said.

"Hi," said Evelyn, Abe's niece, who ran the retail shop for her most days. "Can you come over?" Evelyn, who described herself as "fat, friendly, and over forty," was normally completely unperturbable. Today, however, she sounded perturbed.

"Sure, Ev. Got a problem?"

"In spades! I just sold the last twenty-five bales of peat moss and now Uncle Abe tells me they were on hold for old Mr. Hansen, you know, the guy who grows raspberries out in Hillsboro? The supplier was supposed to have had our new shipment in yesterday, but now he says he won't be able to make it at all today because one truck's broken down and all his others are committed to other places."

"Ha! So he thinks we'll just quietly do without? Okay. I'm on my way." Angrily, Sandy turned off the intercom, then shoved her chair back and got to her feet.

"Darn it, they all seem to think that just because I'm a greenhorn at the business they can get away with things like this. Abe says they never tried to pull such stunts on my grandmother, or if they did, they didn't do it more than once. She was a tough businesswoman by all accounts." She sighed as she slipped her feet into her moccasins. "And all I am is a fake who'd rather be landscaping than dealing with suppliers. But here I go."

"Yup, there you go, leaving your poor house guest to his own devices while you're off tilting at recalcitrant suppliers. Some relationship this is going to be."

She felt a twinge of alarm at his words. "What makes you think there's going to be any kind of relationship?" she asked more sharply than she'd intended.

He wasn't bothered by her tone. He only grinned and said, "Your lips and your arms and your wickedly flirtatious eyes and—"

"And your imagination, which I suggest you curb." In spite of herself Sandy spluttered with laughter. "I don't know how long I'll be, but make yourself at home. Lots of books and magazines in the living room. Thataway." She gestured just before she darted out the back door—in a hurry to get out, so she could hurry back again.

By the time she did get back, though, more than an hour had passed, and when she walked into the house she was met by total silence. The kitchen, to her delight, had been cleaned up. The stove was gleaming and so, too, were the countertop and table. Rick Gearing knew his way around a kitchen. But there was no sign of him.

She checked all the rooms and found him where she should have looked first—in her room, on her bed, fast asleep.

He was sprawled on his back, one hand under his head, the other, palm upward, at his side, half obscured by the front of the robe, which had come untied and fallen open. She dragged in a shaky breath and stared.

He was beautiful. There was no other word for it. Relaxed in sleep, one leg bent slightly to the side, he might have been a carving entitled *Greek God at Rest* except for his slow, even breathing. No, she thought, make it *Norse God.* The golden hair on his chest darkened as it tapered into a V that almost diminished by the time it reached his neatly indented navel. There, it flared out again, darker still, as it shadowed his nested male parts. He was magnificent—the stuff of which fantasies are made. The problem was that her fantasies had been quite graphic enough the past six weeks without a scene like this to add more fuel to them. Quickly snatching up a blanket from the back of her maple rocking chair, she draped it over him. He stirred, and she went rigid, but he only snuggled the cover up under his chin and rolled to his side, facing away from her.

How vulnerable the back of his neck looked, how thickly the hair curled there. Her fingers itched to touch, and it was with great difficulty that she resisted the temptation. Contenting herself with merely smoothing the blanket over his back and shoulders, she tiptoed from the room and closed the door firmly behind her as if locking away something she wasn't prepared to share, not even with her conscious mind.

Rick came slowly awake, aware at first only that he was in a bed that smelled heavenly. Then, light against his eyelids told him it was daylight, and sibilant whispers told him he wasn't alone. Eyes still shut, he lay unmoving, trying to figure out where he was.

"I don't *know*, I said, Pammy," he heard an impatient voice declare. "I guess he could be. He's wearing that thing Mom said belonged to him."

"If he is our dad, I wonder why he came back? Isn't he dead? Maybe he's a ghost."

"More likely he's some guy who just sneaked in. You know how Granny always says Mom should lock the doors to make sure nobody can get into the house. We better go tell Uncle Abe."

"Yeah. Okay. But can we have our snack first? I'm starved."

The door clicked shut and Rick sat up, rubbing his bristly jaw. He yawned, stretched, and decided he felt great. Still clinging to him was the delicate scent of the pillow he'd been hugging. He smiled. No wonder he'd hugged it. It smelled just like that sweet, small armful of woman he'd held in his arms.

Damn, but he was glad those kids didn't have a father lurking somewhere in the nearby bushes, glad the robe he was wearing didn't belong to a live-in boyfriend, glad he was here at last, because Sandy Filmore had captivated him in a parking lot and he knew he would never be the same again. And today, after having kissed her, he felt renewed. Thinking about the softness of her mobile mouth as it played with his, teasing . . . tempting . . . stirring him up madly—

He stood quickly, aware that his thoughts were in danger of creating a reaction he'd prefer not to have two little girls see, to say nothing of their mother, should she have returned to the house. There was a time and a place. And while this might be the right place, it certainly was not the right time.

As the blanket fell from him, he saw that the robe had come untied and was hanging open— Which had come first, the untying, or the covering?

He heard the girls' voices in the kitchen and stepped into the laundry room, finding the clothes in the dryer. He lifted the wad out and folded Sandy's things neatly, his hand lingering on a scrap of pale green lace that couldn't cover more than a quarter of that firm, round little bottom that had fit so well into his cupped palms.

With his own things bundled under one arm, he went into the bathroom, where he dressed quickly and then used her brush to tidy his hair. He ran his tongue over his teeth and looked longingly at the only adult-size toothbrush hanging in the rack. He remembered the sweet taste of her, picked it up, and used it.

He rubbed his whiskery chin once more, searching through the medicine cabinet for a razor, then found a pink plastic one on the side of the tub. He winced at the first stroke of its dull blade. How many times did she shave her legs before putting in a new razor blade? An intriguing picture of Sandy, in the tub, shaving her legs, filled his mind, making him groan softly.

Slow down, he told himself. *There's plenty of time.* But it was going to be damned hard holding back when for six weeks he had wanted her, felt he knew her, had marked her as his own. But it was only in his dreams that he knew her, that she knew him. In reality, they had only just met, and he'd better start trying to remember that.

In the kitchen, a jar of peanut butter, open on the table, a jar of jelly beside it, and a loaf of bread on the counter with several slices hanging out attested to the making of sandwiches. A dirty knife hung balanced precariously on the edge of the table and two saucer-eyed, golden-haired urchins stared at him, one with a sandwich jammed halfway into her mouth. Black lashes, just like their mother's, fringed brilliant blue eyes under arched dark-gold brows.

"Are you our father?" demanded the one without the sandwich, getting to her feet, her tilted chin and aggressive manner amusingly reminiscent of another scared female in a parking lot. She wore a red T-shirt and somewhat grubby jeans with a patch on one knee. Her sneakers were untied.

"No, Jennifer," he said, taking a wild stab in the dark, knowing he had a fifty-fifty chance of being right. "Just a friend."

Her round eyes went even rounder. Her mouth fell open. She shut it with an audible click of her teeth and asked, awed, "How did *you* know which one I am?"

Bingo! he congratulated himself. "You look like a Jennifer," he said easily, leaning in the doorway, smiling at the pair of them.

"I do? But Pammy and I look just the same. Does she look like a Jennifer too?"

"Not at all. She looks like a Pamela." And she did, he realized, with her knee socks, lace-edged blue skirt, and white blouse. "Are you going to leave that mess for your mother to clean up?"

Better, he thought, to change the subject while he was ahead.

"No, sir," said Pamela meekly. She popped the rest of the sandwich into her mouth, stuffed the bread back into the bag, and dropped the knife into the sink.

At a questioning look from Rick, Jennifer hastily put the lid on the peanut butter and put it, along with the jelly, into the refrigerator.

"Where's your mother?" asked Rick, stepping fully into the room to touch the side of the coffeepot, testing for warmth. It was cold. She'd shut it off.

"Here," said Jennifer, reaching on toptoe to get a mug down from a cupboard. "You fill that up and I'll zap it in the microwave for you." He did as he was told and she set the mug inside, shut the door, and punched a series of numbers expertly on the pad. "Seventy seconds is what it takes," she said briskly. "What's your name?"

"Richard Gearing. Where is your mother?" he asked again.

"Who knows?" Jennifer shrugged, grinning. "Out sitting on a stump somewhere, drawing pictures or dreaming. Our mom's a real dreamer, you know."

"I didn't know, but I sort of suspected," he said, sitting down at the table.

"But she doesn't leave us alone, if that's what you think," said Pamela. "We just got home from school. She's usually here when we do, and if she's not, we can go over to the store and be with Evelyn, or out to the greenhouses with Uncle Abe. Granny says mothers can't afford to be dreamers, but I don't agree. I think she's a great mom."

"I'm sure you do," said Rick, suppressing a smile, "and I'm sure she's a fine mom." Gentle Pamela was so unlike her sister in personality that he didn't think they could be called identical. But if they were not dressed so differently, or if they were sleeping . . .

"She'll be back soon," Pamela promised.

"Probably," he agreed. "She may be out looking for my car keys."

Jennifer gave a shout of laughter. "Your car keys? Did Never get them? He loves keys. His last name is More. Mom says it's from a poem, but I think it's because he always wants more. More toys, more food, more stroking." The microwave had given a sharp beep while she was talking. Now she opened the door and passed Rick his coffee.

"Sugar and milk?" asked Pam.

He shook his head with a smile of thanks.

Jennifer watched him sip in silence for several moments and then said suspiciously, "Do we have to call you Uncle Richard?"

"No, of course not. Just Rick will do."

"Oh, good. Then you're not Mom's boyfriend?"

"Jen, that's rude," Pamela said gently, sadly.

He grinned at Jenny. "Wouldn't you like your mom to have a boyfriend?" It was nice, he thought, to know that she obviously didn't—at least not one the girls knew about.

Jennifer, hovering between cupboards and table, gave him a baleful look. "My best friend

Sheena's mom has a boyfriend and Sheena has to call him Uncle Todd. He sleeps in her mom's room and her and her little brother can't get into bed with their mom in the mornings anymore because there's not enough room."

"That's too bad," he commiserated, wishing he could reassure her that if he were ever fortunate enough to spend nights in her mother's bed there'd be plenty of room left over for wriggling kids in the morning. He'd been one himself once and remembered how good and warm and secure early morning snuggles had made him feel.

"So how come you were sleepin' in Mom's bed?" demanded the aggressive twin. She stood there, hands on hips, waiting, chin tilted high, and he wanted to hug her.

"I wasn't sleeping in it, just on it. There's a difference, you know."

"What difference?"

He opened his mouth and then shut it again, shrugging. "There is one. Trust me, okay? There is, but I can't quite explain it. I was taking a nap because I drove all night and I was tired. When I got here, Never swiped my keys and I couldn't go to a motel to sleep."

"But you were undressed," insisted Jennifer. "You were wearing our father's nightie."

He couldn't help laughing. "That, my lady, was no nightie. Men don't wear nighties. It was a bathrobe, and that, too, is a difference I can't explain," he added quickly as Jennifer, her eyes gleaming, opened her mouth again.

"How come you can't explain things?" asked Pam. Then, kindly, she offered: "I could ask Mom to teach you. She explained my arithmetic to me."

Before Rick could respond to that, Jennifer swept on. She had a bone in her teeth and she was not going to let it go. "How come you had to get all undressed if you were just taking a nap?"

"Because my clothes got wet and with everything I own locked up in my car and my keys flying around somewhere with Never, I needed something to wear while your mother dried my clothes."

"How did your clothes get wet?" Jenny perched herself on a chair, looking as if she might sit still for a minute provided he entertained her with an interesting story.

"I fell in the creek. No, that's not entirely true. The creek fell on me."

"And that, I suppose," said Jennifer, frighteningly adult for an instant, "is another difference you can't explain?"

"Oh, no," he said with a grin. "That one I can handle. Your mother did it. She unplugged a dam and spilled an entire waterfall down over my head."

"Figures," said Jenny. "Mom likes building dams and things."

"She is a landscape designer," said Pamela gravely. "Part of her job is to move water around."

"What were you doing in the creek?" Jenny was clearly interested. "I fell in, too, my first day here. I was trying to catch a duck."

He had just opened his mouth to start explaining when a slight noise behind him made him turn. He got to his feet and smiled down at Sandy, who stood in the doorway, clutching a sketchbook to her breast, a flush tinting her face and her breath rushing in and out as if she'd been running.

"Oh!" she said breathlessly. "You're awake. I hurried when I realized what time it was, hoping I could get back and keep the girls quiet while you slept." She hugged her daughters close and said, "I'm sorry I wasn't here when you got home, kids. Do you want a snack?"

"We had it already," said Pam.

Sandy's eyes swept the kitchen. "Where's the mess?"

"Rick made us clean it up."

"Jenny! You know better than to call adults by their first name. It's Doc . . . Mr. Gearing."

"But he told us to call him Rick and he told us to clean up our mess."

"Since when have you been so willing to do what you're told?"

Jenny grinned unrepentantly. "You always said I was very obedient when I wanted to do what I was told to do."

"The way I put it is that you are obedient when you're told to do what you want to do. There is a difference. I think." Only it was increasingly difficult to think while Rick stood there smiling at her, much too big for the confines of this small kitchen.

"Like the difference between sleeping in a bed and on it, and the difference between a nightie and a bathrobe?"

Sandy stared at Jennifer, then narrowed her gaze on Rick, who smiled blandly. "Something tells me not to go into that right now," she said, sinking onto a chair at the table.

"Okay," Jenny said cheerfully. "Can we go out and play now?"

"Of course."

Pam leaned against Sandy's shoulder. "That's okay, Mom. We can stay and help you be polite to Mr. Gearing."

"Does your mother often need help being polite?" Rick asked, sitting back down and ignoring the black look he got from Sandy.

"No, not always," said Pam loyally. "But when the church ladies came, she made us stay and help her. Would you like to see some of my books, Mr. Gearing?"

"Pammy! He *said* we could call him *Rick*!" Jenny said from the doorway. "Now, come on. I think he and Mom would like to be alone." She darted across the room and grabbed her twin by the hand, dragging her to the door while Sandy was still staring, jaw agape.

"What for?" Pam asked plaintively. "Why do they want to be alone?"

"I'll tell you if you come *now*."

Pammy went.

Sandy stared down at the table for a long time

before she looked up to see Rick's laughing eyes on her.

"I'd really like to eavesdrop on that conversation," he said, but Sandy only continued to look bewildered. He wondered if her children often had that effect on her. He'd felt like that sometimes with Roger. She reached over and touched the coffeepot.

"You fill this," Rick said gently, handing her a mug. "I'll zap it in the microwave for you. Seventy seconds is what it takes."

She nodded absently, her mind clearly elsewhere, and then looked at him sharply. "That sounded like a quote. I suppose Jenny's been bossing you around. She does it to me too."

"Bossing me and grilling me and telling me all about you and your foibles. Pam, of course, championed you every chance she got. I like your kids, Sandy. I like them a lot."

She only looked at him, then at the table, till her coffee was hot. He handed her the cup, lifted his own half-full one, and clicked it against hers.

"What are you drinking to?"

"Friendship," he said easily, "and whatever else might develop." His eyes told her he expected those developments to be rapid and vast.

She felt a surge of something forbidden inside herself and murmured, "Friendship," while looking at him speculatively, her eyes unintentionally provocative as she gazed at him over the rim of her mug.

Or was it so unintentional, he wondered, seeing a little flare of what could be excitement in those brown depths. He waited until she had set her cup down before saying casually, "By the way, thanks for covering me with that blanket."

He was rewarded, and his earlier question answered, by the dusky rose flush that tinged her cheeks, and by the flicker of guilt that crossed her face. Her tongue came out, pink and dainty, to moisten her lower lip. He knew that the robe had been untied when she covered him, and knew that she'd liked what she'd seen, even if she wasn't ready to admit it.

"You're welcome," she said a trifle hoarsely. "I didn't want the kids to come home and find you like . . . that."

He chuckled. "You could have stood guard."

Suddenly, she grinned, impish and purely delightful. "I didn't dare. You, Richard Gearing, have a magnificent body and you know it. And yes," she added challengingly, daring him to comment. "I looked. And given the opportunity, wouldn't you have done exactly the same?"

"Me?" he asked, amazed. "Hell, no. I get a chance to look at that body in the mirror anytime I want. It doesn't impress me much anymore."

She laughed, a pretty sound that lingered even as she said, "You know what I mean."

"Yes, I know what you mean, and all right, if our positions had been reversed, I'd have looked, too, and probably done a lot more than just that."

For an instant there was a tremulousness about her mouth and that flare of excitement in her eyes before she damped it.

"I used your toothbrush," he said. "It tasted as sweet as you did." He held her startled gaze for as long as he dared, knowing he was on the verge of reaching across the table and kissing her until they both melted. In order to give himself something else to think about, if it were possible, he switched his gaze to her sketchbook and reached for it instead.

She tried to snatch it from his gasp. "Hey, no. My toothbrush, okay, since we'd swapped saliva anyway. But leave my sketchbook alone."

He held on, refusing to budge. "Swapped saliva? Is that what you call it? Is that the best you can do to describe an experience that was so beautiful it was almost . . . holy?"

She laughed breathlessly. "Somehow, I can't believe you were having holy thoughts while we were kissing."

His laugh was a pleasant bass rumble. "And you are absolutely right." Deftly, he twisted the sketchbook out of her hands and flipped it open.

He leafed through it, his expression going from mild interest to wide-eyed disbelief. "Is this my place? It is, isn't it?" She nodded, half embarrassed, and reached for her book again.

"Just wait," he said, and leafed through again, more slowly, before closing it with a snap and saying, "Do it."

"Do . . . do what?"

"My property. Landscape it. I like your plan. It's what I want."

"Are you out of your mind? That's just one of my fantasies you see there, a game I play with myself, pretending I have a contract to landscape a big, beautiful acreage."

"You've got one."

"One what?"

"A contract." He reached across the table with his right hand, wrapped hers in it, and shook it briefly but firmly. "There," he said. "We've shaken on it. A gentleman's agreement. And my word is as good as my money, Ms. Filmore."

"But that's just it," she said, wild hope at war with common sense. Of course he didn't mean it. Or, if he did, he would change his mind. Her design for his place would cost a lot to realize. For one thing, there was that waterfall.

"What's just it?"

"Money. It might run into more than you're willing to pay. In dreaming, I never make myself hold back."

"So cost it out." He shrugged. "If I think you're going overboard, I'll haul you back in."

"Do you mean it? Honestly?"

"I mean it, Sandy. Honestly." Those expressive brown eyes glowed and then glistened with a sheen he hoped wouldn't well up and overflow. It didn't. She had to blink a couple of times, and sniff unobtrusively, but then she laughed, a delighted gurgle that made him feel like a hero. Her hero.

Getting to her feet, she fished in her shorts pockets and pulled out a key ring, dangling it before him. "A prime consideration in the landscaping of a residential property is the view from within the dwelling," she said, lecturer-style. "Mr. Gearing, would you be so good as to show me around your house?"

He snatched the keys as he got to his feet, capturing her fingers along with them. "Where did you get these, and when?"

"Never dropped them at my feet when I was on my way up the hill."

He withdrew his hand, leaving the keys dangling from her fingers, and touched her cheek softly. "Why don't you give them back to him?"

Sandy felt the whisper of his touch on her skin, all the way down to her toes, and stepped back from him with difficulty. "Because," she said, meeting his sober gaze with one of equal solemnity. "Just because."

Then quickly, she turned and picked up her sketchbook and led the way out of the house.

Four

"When I saw this on the sketches, I had no idea how well it was really going to work," Rick said, standing beside Sandy on the upper level of the property, where now a narrow stream wandered across from one side to the other. Diverted from the main creek, it cascaded down on the west side, where the high bluff was shallowest, and continued in a lazy but broader sweep across the lower level in front of the house. It then flowed through a culvert under the drive and back into the main stream, depriving Sandy, the downstream neighbor, of nothing much at all. But taking half the flow and redirecting it this way had reduced the force of the waterfall, so the quiet of the master bedroom wasn't shattered. Now only a tame splashing came down the rock face to keep the pool filled with liquid crystal. It was what Sandy had proposed to the developer who had pooh-poohed her ideas, calling them "female impracticalities."

"It's like a miracle," Rick went on.

"Nothing miraculous about it," she said as she moved to the brink to wave the backhoe operator in a wider circle where he was leveling a mound of soil.

"But in only five days, you've accomplished so much," Rick said. "I hardly recognize the place. Yet as much as you've done, it still looks natural and . . . well, countrylike, I guess I'd have to say."

"Good. I'm glad you're pleased. It would be a shame to have five acres of woodland and snatch it all bald just to plant ornamental trees the way so many people do. I think our native trees are pretty ornamental too. Especially the cedars. They're so lacy, yet strong, and they're always shaped so elegantly."

She paused, watching the backhoe as it growled and moved and shifted earth from one place to another. "Are you certain you don't want a pond down there at the bottom?" she asked wistfully. "Then Roger could have ducks."

Rick laughed. "You and your ponds. I'm certain I don't want one. If Roger wants to play with ducks, he can go and play with yours." He tilted her chin up and looked into her eyes. "Can't he?"

"Of course he can." Uncomfortable with the intensity of his gaze, she looked down and moved

away from him. Rick seemed to think that Roger
was going to fit right in. But she was worried.

How could she tell Rick to cool it when there
was really nothing to cool? There wasn't. There
couldn't be. Yet, given even the slightest encour-
agement, she knew her heart could quickly learn
to need Rick Gearing. There hadn't been any en-
couragement, though. Since that first day, their
touching and kissing had been kept to a bare
minimum. Once in a while he could stroke her
cheek, or catch her chin to turn her face up to his
as he had just moments before. Even more rarely,
he would drop a casual kiss onto her nose or her
cheek, but—respecting her wishes, wishes never
really expressed but which he seemed to understand anyway—never in front of the kids. She was
grateful; if a relationship were to develop between
them, however unlikely it seemed, she felt it would
have to be kept apart from her children's lives.
And apart from his son's life too. She didn't think
it would be fair to involve children in something
that was doomed to end.

Taking her hand, Rick walked toward a new
flight of stone stairs, flanked with flowering shrubs,
which had been built beside the bubbling cascade
of the new section of stream.

"Don't," she said, trying to pull her hand free.
"I'm filthy."

He held her hand tighter. "I don't care. I'm wash-
able." She stopped struggling. It was nice to feel

her hand nestled in his as they walked down to the main level of the grounds. It was even nicer when he slipped free and put his arm over her shoulder as they ascended the slope toward the house.

"Have you come up with a name for your new business yet?"

Sandy didn't hesitate. "Oh, yes. Aabab Landscaping."

He lifted his brows. "Aabab? Why not Filmore?"

She laughed. "You just said it. "Fill-more Landscaping? Awful. Conjures up a picture of huge dump trucks unloading quantities of questionable material for me to plant grass over. No, thanks. I'll take Aabab. Besides, Aabab Landscaping can hang quite nicely on the coattails of Aabab Nursery Gardens and still come first in the yellow pages in its category."

She paused at the edge of the driveway, where her battered pickup stood, and tilted her head back to look up at him. "I've been seriously thinking about taking my own name back for personal as well as professional use. What do you think of Sandy Aabab? Sounds better than Sandy Filmore?"

"Oh, absolutely," he said, enchanted as always by this sprite of a woman with her big, earnest brown eyes, and willing to agree to anything she said—except waiting for her to get over being afraid of what was clearly happening between them.

"Good. I always hated having to change my

name," she confided. "Not that I was all that close to my father. In fact, we weren't close at all, but it just didn't seem fair that I should have to become somebody else because I had to marry Alex Filmore." She frowned. "Especially when I didn't want to."

He frowned, too, and looked down at her. "What do you mean, *had* to?"

She shrugged and looked uncomfortable. "I mean what that normally means."

He shook his head and put his hands on her waist, lifting her to sit on the open tailgate of the truck. "Come on. Even in the dark ages nine years ago, nobody *had* to get married for that reason."

"Believe me," she said, "I had to. You didn't know my father."

"You said you didn't want to. Your father made you marry a man you didn't love?"

"Let's simply say the pressure was too great for a naive and scared twenty-year-old to withstand. And besides, when I let Alex make love to me, I really believed we were in love with each other. It wasn't until I thought about spending my life with him that I knew all I had felt was . . . well, curiosity, and the strong sexual drive of the young. But I was pregnant and terrified and so very, very ashamed, and I let myself be bulldozed into marrying him. I had no resources of any kind. I'd had only two years of college. I was more or less unemployable, especially pregnant. And my dad wouldn't help me. To put it mildly, he wasn't pleased with me. I had shamed him, you see." She stared at the ground, thinking what a hypocrite her father was. He'd hardly been simon-pure.

Rick slipped his hand behind her head, under the heavy thickness of her dark braid which had fallen from the high roll she usually wore it in. Her skin was warm and damp and soft. "What about your mother?"

"She died just before I turned thirteen. And even if she'd been alive, I don't suppose she'd have been much help. She was totally dominated by my father. We both were. He didn't even want me to go to college, but I won a full scholarship, so he couldn't really stop me once I turned eighteen."

"And what about the girls' father? Did he want to marry you?"

Sandy glanced up for a moment and laughed mirthlessly. "Are you kidding? He was furious. All he did was complain about how I'd ruined his life. He had to quit school, too, of course, and go to work. After the babies were born, I would have gotten some kind of work so he could go back to school, but he was one of those men who bristle violently at the idea of wives going out to work."

Even wives they hate, she thought, remembering the years of Alex telling her she was useless, a parasite, a drag. Later she'd come to understand he'd wanted to keep her jobless, dependent upon him for everything. It gave him immense power over her. Her place, he seemed to think, was squarely under his thumb, a victim of his total contempt. How many times had he called her a whore? She'd lost count. For a while maybe she'd even accepted his belief that marriage was nothing more than a form of legalized prostitution. He had used her sexually all the while saying he really didn't want her.

"Why don't you leave me alone, then?" she remembered asking one night when he had finished with her and had started berating her for a lousy performance.

"Because you're bought and paid for," he'd snarled. "And, baby, don't you ever forget what you've cost me—my youth, my freedom, my education, my future. And now you can't even give me sons!"

It did no good to remind him that they had two lovely little daughters; he didn't care about the girls. All he seemed to be able to remember was that in giving birth to the twins, she had been damaged and had to have surgery. There would be no more children.

How she had loathed him even while she feared him. And then, finally, after nearly five years of hell, he had walked out on her, and she had felt nothing but relief.

"The girls said that their father had died." Rick's voice cut into her thoughts. "Did he, or is that what you told them to make his absence easier for them?"

"He's dead," she replied, finally looking up at

him. "About a month after the final decree, he wrapped himself and his motorcycle around a tree."

Rick was quiet for several moments while his fingers played comfortingly over the muscles in the back of her neck and her upper shoulders. "Did you feel a great sense of loss?" he asked at last. "I mean, during the time you were together, did you come to care for him?"

Sandy shook her head. "There's no way to love someone who thinks you're nothing but a parasite," she said. "He stayed for as long as it suited his purposes. When he left, I was relieved, even though we had to live on macaroni and cheese and powdered milk for a long time. When he left, he stopped supporting us. I did get a job, then, but I wasn't equipped to earn much.

"His parents didn't know he hadn't been supporting us, and after his death they took over what they saw as his responsibility toward his children. I accepted their help. I had to. They loaned me enough money to finish my education and looked after the girls for me. I . . . owe them a lot."

What she didn't say was that she was still paying them back and would be for a long, long time, especially if she couldn't make the nursery pay the way her grandmother had.

Hopping down from the back of the truck, she gave Rick a cheerful, friendly smile. "I have to go now. The kids will be home any minute and I have an evening's worth of invoices to check and bills to pay. See you tomorrow."

"Not so fast," he said, capturing her hand. "What if I take all three of you out for dinner tonight? The way you work, you shouldn't have to cook after you get home."

Sandy had to laugh, thinking of how little cooking she actually did. She and the girls ate a lot of salads and ordered out for pizza much too often. "Sounds great," she said, swinging the tailgate shut so the shovels and rakes wouldn't fall out. Opening the door of the pickup, she got behind the wheel. "The kids will love it. They don't get to go out very often. Pam still talks about what she calls 'our date' with Mr. Lawson. He teaches at the college and asked me out one night last fall. I completely forgot that I even had a date, and when he showed up, it was too late to get a sitter. Since I couldn't leave the girls, I suggested we take them along."

She laughed again, remembering. "He said he didn't mind, but how he lied! He hated it and was so rude that we couldn't believe it. He sat and glowered all evening, and tried to ruin our enjoyment of the meal. We didn't let him, of course, and I'm glad, because that was 'our' last date with Mr. Lawson, believe me. On the way home he tried to grope me in the front seat—with my children right there in the back!"

Rick laughed sympathetically. "I promise. No glowering and no groping."

She was quite certain that nothing this man ever did to a woman would be inept enough to be called "groping." "Thanks," she said. "I'd appreciate it."

He looked at her for several beats before saying in a low growl, "And I would appreciate a kiss, Sandy *Aabab*." She smiled at the sound of her own name on his lips. Somehow, it took away the bad taste of using Alex Filmore's name for so long.

Bending and putting his head inside the cab of the truck, Rick touched her lips with his. Hers parted as if by instinct and permitted his tongue to slide inside, where it stroked softly, then strongly. Her head spun, her stomach fluttered, and a small, pleasured sound escaped from her throat.

He lifted his head for an instant, murmured her name as he looked into her glowing eyes, and then kissed her again, more deeply, putting his hands under her arms and around her back. Suddenly, a loud, blaring sound broke them apart and he jumped back, startled, banging his head on the door frame while Sandy jerked her elbow off the horn.

Rick laughed. "I've heard of seeing colored lights and hearing ringing bells, but that was a new one on me." He gave her one more very quick kiss and then shut the door. "Go," he said, "before I forget all my good intentions long before I mean to."

Sandy went, but thought as she turned right at the end of his driveway that whatever his intentions might be, and however difficult it was going to be to withstand them, she was going to have to. Clearly, they wouldn't be good for her . . . and the firm plan she had for her life.

"Oh, Rick!" Sandy jumped out of the truck the next morning and stood gazing at the big, freshly painted sign that stood at the front of his property. A slope of green grass, a swath of blue sky, and a branch of rhododendrons with bright red flowers provided a background for the neatly scrolled letters which spelled out LANDSCAPING BY AABAB. Rick, a wooden mallet in one hand, had just finished pounding the signposts into the soil.

"Oh, Rick," she said again, looking at his paint-smeared jeans and shirt. "You did that for me?"

"Of course I did," he said, leaning the mallet against the back of the sign and drawing her loosely into an embrace. "I like doing things for you. You're a very worthy recipient."

"And you're a very nice man," she said, sliding her hands up his chest to his shoulders, coming up on tiptoe to kiss him gently on the lips. "Thank you. The sign's just beautiful."

"I told you last night that you'd need to advertise in order to get more contracts. This is one way to go about it. People driving by will see what miracles you've wrought here and start hammering on your door."

She smiled wistfully. "That would be great, wouldn't it?"

"It'll happen," he said confidently, and dipped his head to kiss her. She parted her lips slightly to his pressure and then backed off, feeling surging heat through her body, heat she didn't want to feel.

"You sound so sure," she said in a wobbly voice that turned into a husky whisper as he pulled her back against his body. "Rick—"

"I am sure," he said thickly, his lips on her once more. "As sure as I am that this is right for us, Sandy."

"But . . ." But it isn't, she had been going to say—only all at once she wasn't totally convinced it wasn't. His kisses were perfect. Each one was different. And each one had the power to stir her more deeply than she had ever been stirred before. What, she wondered, would happen to her if she were to permit him to take those kisses to their natural conclusion? She felt herself melting as she thought about it. What would it be like, making love to a man this gentle, yet this passionate? A man she liked as well as she liked Rick? It would be different, so very, very different . . .

Rick lifted his head, looked down at her, his blue eyes dark with desire. In his throat a pulse hammered wildly and she gave in to the impulse to feel the heavy throbbing power of his blood surging beneath the skin she tasted with the tip of her tongue. She raised her face to his again, and her hands to the back of his head. "Rick . . ." she heard herself whisper raggedly as her lips parted invitingly. She knew she should stop, knew she should step away from him, but the urge to get closer was stronger than common sense. This was now, and now was all she could think about as she drew in the scent of his body, felt his lips hard and demanding as they forced hers farther apart, felt the urgent thrust of his tongue deep into her mouth and the even more urgent thrust of his body as he cupped her buttocks and held her tightly in the cradle of his thighs.

"Sandy . . ." His eyes were unfocused and his breathing was as ragged as hers when she pulled back from him. Against her lower body, his hardness pulsed, thrilling her, scaring her, building a want in her that she knew she would never stop feeling. "Dear Lord, you have potent kisses! More," he said. "I need more. Touch me. Put your hands on my skin . . . ah, there, like that," he murmured as she stroked his neck and throat. "So cool, so smooth, like angel's hands." Then their lips joined again as their arms strained to pull each other closer, tighter, their bodies moving with an age-old rhythm they couldn't begin to deny.

Sandy was flying, soaring, rising high on a heated current, her whole body alive as it never had been before. She took his head in her hands, at last permitting herself the luxury of stroking her fingers into the thickness of his hair, running it between them over and over, feeling the shape of his skull, the curve of his ears, the hammering pulse in his throat, again and again, and finally, the mat of hair on his chest.

Against his chest her breasts swelled, nipples hardening inside her clothing until she thought she would scream with the need to have them soothed by his mouth and tongue and stroking hands. He tore himself away from her and set her back, hands trembling on her arms.

"Wow!" He breathed against her forehead before he stepped back completely, his hands balled into fists at his side. "Do you have any idea of the danger you present to the men of this world? You should be locked up in somebody's vault."

From the ardent look in his eyes, she could guess whose vault he had in mind. "Doesn't sound like much fun to me," she said lightly. "I'd hate to be locked up." Knees still weak, she sat down on one of the big cedar logs that formed a border at the side of the road.

Rick joined her. He frowned at her words, and said, his tone anything but light, "I promise, Sandy, that no matter what, I won't make you feel locked up. Ever."

She shook her head. "Promises are . . . well, a bit premature, I'd say. And quite unnecessary."

"Are they?"

She nodded. "Promises are for people who are planning a future together. And we are not," she added firmly.

"Dammit, you can't go on pretending that nothing's happening between us, that there isn't a future, or at least the very strong possibility of a future together for us. And I don't think it's too early for me to make sure you know that I'd never try to tie you down to a life you didn't want. That's all I was trying to say."

"There is no possible future for us," she said. "As anything but friends. Rick . . . I can't . . . couldn't begin to have a relationship with you. Not the way things are."

"No? And how are things?"

"I'm in debt. Deeply in debt. I have to pay back the Filmores for my education. The two years I was in school they paid my rent, gave me an allowance for groceries and clothing for myself and the girls, looked after them for me so I didn't have to hire a sitter, and paid for my tuition and books. It was a whole lot of money, believe me. I've been chipping away at it, but it's not easy. Back in Ohio I worked as a landscaper for Rance Developments, and the pay wasn't great. When I inherited the nursery, I thought things would ease up financially, but it hasn't worked out that way. My grandmother was quite sick the last few years and things sort of went downhill, I guess. So I'm not only learning how to run the business, I have a lot of lost ground to make up as well."

"Couldn't you have sold the nursery and ended up ahead of the game?" he asked.

Slowly, reluctantly, she nodded. "I suppose so. But the minute I saw it, I knew I couldn't do that. For the first time in my life I felt I belonged somewhere. Here. And then there's Abe."

Briefly, she told him of Abe's relationship with her late grandmother. "He should own the nursery, by rights, and it should go in turn to Evelyn, his niece, and her children. So morally, it isn't mine to sell. No, somehow I have to make it pay, or make the landscaping business pay enough so that I can hire someone knowledgeable to run it for me . . . for Abe and Evelyn. It may be years before I'm free to—" She broke off, shaking her head.

"To what? Fall in love?" he asked, half angry.

"Rick!" Her eyes went wide in alarm. "I don't think . . . I won't . . ."

"Why not, Sandy? Why does it terrify you to think that you could fall in love? It doesn't scare me to think I'm on the verge of falling in love with you. I know I want you, but I believe it's a whole lot bigger and more important than just a physical attraction between the two of us. Did you ever ask yourself how the stranger from the parking lot eventually came to be your next door neighbor?"

"I have wondered," she admitted.

"I'm here, I bought this house, for one reason only—because you are here." She gave him a skeptical look, and he went on. "When I started looking for houses, I told the real estate agent what area I wanted to live in. You'd described your view that night in the bar. You'd dropped other information about your home, too. When I saw this place, saw the two rivers meeting below the house, saw that green hill shaped like a locomotive, and the mountain off to the North, I was sure I was in the vicinity of your place. What capped it was that the realtor told me the woman who ran the nursery just down the hill freaked out over water rights. He didn't know your name but said that yours was the only nursery in the neighborhood. And I knew you owned a nursery. So, even though the house was too big for one man and a boy, even though it was too far from the college, and even though it had a roaring waterfall outside the master bedroom, I bought it. Because of you."

"That's preposterous!" she exclaimed jumping to her feet and gathering an armload of tools out of the back of the truck. "I don't believe you."

She strode away then, leaving him behind, not that he made any attempt to follow. She marched up the stairs beside the stream to the upper level and began laying out pegs and strings where she planned to have a small gazebo built.

"Crazy man," she said to herself later when she was calm enough to think coherently. "Nobody buys a house in an expensive, exclusive neighborhood, where the lots are sized at a minimum of five acres, just because a woman he likes lives downstream. Nobody! And he is no more on the verge of falling in love with me than I am of falling in love with him. It's sex, nothing but sex, and I won't have it!"

"Sex, sex, sex, sexy broad, sexy broad, gimmee a kiss, sexy broad," said a voice nearby, and Sandy got to her feet, rubbing the small of her back.

"Take off, you. If you hadn't swiped his keys in the first place, I wouldn't have had to invite him home with me and none of this would have happened."

Five

"How did you get in here?" Sandy gasped and came abruptly erect on the high-backed bench that sat under a hooded arbor over which climbed a profusion of sweetbrier roses. "That gate's been locked since day before yesterday." He had come down the back way. She knew that, because she would have heard his footsteps in the gravel if he'd come up the driveway.

He grinned as he sat down beside her, too close, and handed her the key to the padlock. "Were you trying to keep me out? You left this in the lock."

Sandy stared at the key on her hand. "Oh. That was stupid of me, wasn't it?"

"Freud would have found it interesting," he said, cupping her face with his hand. "Don't be scared, Sandy. And don't try to lock me out. You'll have about as much success as I'd have if I tried to lock you up."

"Rick . . ." She leaned into his hand, trapping it for a moment between her cheek and her shoulder before lifting her head. He turned his palm down and caressed her fine bones. "I really am scared."

"I know that. But I don't know why. Can you tell me?"

Instead of answering his question, she asked one of her own. "Rick, why did you take Roger away from his mother?"

He released her hand and sat forward, elbows on his knees, hands dangling between his legs. He remained silent for so long she thought he wasn't going to tell her. Then, in a subdued voice, he said, "I didn't."

"But you—"

"No. You misunderstood and I didn't correct you. Elaine gave Roger up voluntarily. She didn't want him anymore." Rick lifted his head and stared into her eyes, his face harsh and bleak in the twilight. "I was a Sunday father. That was all I was permitted to be, of course, but I never fought for more. I could have. I should have. But always I told myself that I'd demand more time with my son when he was older, when we could do more together, when I was less pressured at work, when we could enjoy each other more. I told myself that it was better for Roger if I left things the way they were. And maybe it was. But the fact remains, I hardly knew him. Worse, he hardly knew me. Then one Sunday afternoon when I went to the house to get him for our customary three and a half hours together, Elaine met me at the door with a semi-hysterical child and all his belongings neatly packed. She had told him he had to live with me, and the poor little guy was terrified."

Sandy moaned, and the sound was full of pain, while her expression registered the horror she felt. Rick stroked her cheek gently. This woman, he knew, could never be cruel to a child.

"Elaine was getting married and her new husband travels. That was the only explanation she gave me—or Roger. I took him, of course. He's my son, and I love him. But my apartment had no bed for him, no space for him to play, nothing familiar to him at all. And he had just turned four. He stood at the door, his eyes pleading with me to open it and take him home. He didn't talk to me, he just . . . looked at me, and I knew he hated me. When it really penetrated that he was separated from his mother, from the one person he adored, he blamed me, hated me for taking him away from his mother. And he cried. For three days and nights, it seemed, he cried constantly. I tried to call Elaine. I couldn't locate her. I was frantic, but so was my son.

"I got him to eat, but he threw up. For three days he lived on ginger ale—and on my lap. Even though he hated me, and wouldn't talk to me, he needed an adult for comfort. All I could do was hold him and rock him and try to make him feel safe. But it wasn't enough. I wasn't enough."

His voice cracked and she reached for him, gathering him close, holding his head against her breasts as she would hold one of her daughters who needed comforting. "Oh, Rick, that poor, poor baby," she whispered, rocking him. Rick's arms slid around her torso, and he held her as he went on.

"On the fourth morning he finally talked to me. I had given up hope that he ever would, and then, when he did, it broke my heart. He looked up at me and said, 'I want my mommy.' And right then, I realized that even though I was a man of thirty-five, I wanted my mommy too.

"Within hours we were on a plane to Hawaii and only a few days after that, a changed little boy was laughing and playing and eating and sleeping like a fairly normal child. My mother has the power of healing, magic in her personality. You see, Roger knew my mother even less than he knew me, but it didn't seem to matter. She fixed him right up."

Sandy slipped her arms from around him and he lifted his head slowly, reluctantly, from her breasts, and when he was sitting up, she found she missed his warmth. "She must be a wonderful woman," she said quickly. "Tell me about her."

He did so, and she could hear the love and admiration in his tone.

"She and Dad had the kind of relationship that makes divorce lawyers gnash their teeth in anticipation of losing their summer homes to foreclosure. Mom says they were in love in many former lives. They married when she was eighteen and he was twenty. I came along a year later, and my brother, Roger, two years after that. Then came Sharon and Sue. They're also two years apart, but there's only eleven months between Roger and Sharon.

"They raised us in a big, rambling house about ten miles from Cape Canaveral, where Dad worked. Then, just when we had all grown up and they had begun to enjoy the freedom and time together, Dad died. That was ten years ago. For a few months we were afraid Mom just might will herself to follow him, but she pulled out of it and decided to make a life for herself. She was only forty-four and there were a lot of years left to enjoy."

He laughed softly and put an arm around Sandy, drawing her head onto his shoulder, draping an arm over her front, holding her there.

"And how she's enjoying those years," he went on. "I was thinking of getting married, Sharon already had, and Susie was in college while Roger was never home except for brief visits. He's an airline pilot. So with all of us dispersed, she sold the house and moved herself to Hawaii. She has a condo in Hilo with a view that kings would kill for and leads a busy life with a full circle of friends. She's turned herself into an interior decorator and is something of a latter-day hippie. She wears patched jeans and old shirts that she filches from my brother or me if either of us is dumb enough to take one off in her presence. Yet, on occasion, she can dress like an Egyptian queen or come up with the most outrageous rigs of her own design."

He turned Sandy in his arms so that she rested half across his lap, her cheek pillowed on his chest, one of his legs bent, providing a resting spot for her arm. She saw his frown and wiped it away gently with one fingertip between his brows before she brought her hand back quickly. Touching him was entirely too addictive.

"Elaine . . . Elaine hated her," he said with a sigh.

"I'm not going to hate her, Rick," she said comfortingly, and then felt the world shift beneath her.

What had she said? What had she done? Why had she drawn that parallel between herself and Elaine?

She withdrew from his embrace and got to her feet, pacing to the edge of the pond, her heart hammering hard in her chest. In saying that, hadn't she as good as made some vague kind of commitment to him? She'd acknowledged that it might matter what she thought of his mother. And why? Was she in danger of acknowledging even more?

Shaking, she felt his hands on her shoulders and let him turn her to face him.

If he thought her statement had been significant, he didn't say so. He only said, "I hope you won't, Sandy. But she's different."

"How different?"

"Oh, so many ways. She's flamboyant. And noisy. And bossy."

"I like flowers," she said, "and they're flamboyant. I love my kids, and Lord knows, they're noisy. And I don't have to let her boss me. I think you worry too much."

"I . . . oh, hell!" He looked like a man who had a terrible confession to make and needed to get it over with. "Sandy, she smokes *cigars*."

Sandy clapped her hand over her mouth, a gust of laughter welling up in spite of Rick's tortured expression. It spurted out and she collapsed onto the grass at his feet, howling, one arm across her eyes. "Cigars? Cigars? Oh, Rick, I'm going to *love* her!"

He stared down at her for a moment before flopping down at her side, hauling her bodily into his arms, suddenly laughing as hard as she. "You know," he said, his voice joyous, "I think you're just crazy enough that you will."

He rolled up on one elbow and looked at her in the light shining from the kitchen window. "And she is going to love you, Sandy. Because . . ." His voice became hushed and his tone sure, so very sure. "Because I do. I love you. Oh, how I love you!"

He gave her no chance to reply, taking her mouth in a bruising kiss that went on and on, his tongue plunging deep, his hands on her body finding the most sensitive places, his thumbs rubbing her nipples until she cried out with the beautiful agony of it. As she strained against him, he slid her shirred tube top down and laved her breasts with his tongue, finally taking her nipple into his mouth.

"Oh, Rick." She heard her own voice come faintly, high and thin, as she locked her fingers into his thick hair and held his head to her breasts.

There was such heavenly pain in his touch, in the sucking, the flicking of his tongue, such ecstasy that she begged for more, silently now, arching her back.

On and on it went, his gentle assault on her senses. Her breathing was short and shallow, her eyes closed, sobs of need rising in her chest. This was unlike anything she had ever experienced, unlike anything she had ever even imagined. Something was happening inside her body that she wasn't able to control.

"I want . . . I want . . ." she said in that faint, far away voice. "I need to touch you too." She gasped. "Rick, help me."

"Mmm." His soft sound was one of agreement, and he eased back so her trembling fingers could attack the buttons of his shirt, and then she was stroking the silky hair on his chest, the smooth skin, the iron muscles underneath. "That feels so good," he said roughly. "Oh, love, I've wanted this for so long."

Slowly, his hands stroked over her body as he leaned above her, cupping her breasts, molding their shapes in his palms, then spanning her narrow waist, moving out over the flare of her hips. Her body pulsed with need, ached for release, for relief from this deep, yearning need, this total hunger he had aroused, and when one of his hands cupped the mound between her thighs, she lifted against it, her knees falling apart even as her eyes fell shut and she cried out to him.

"Please . . . please, Rick."

"Steady, my love, my darling," he told her, getting to his knees and pulling up her top before lifting her into his arms. He paused to kiss her deeply again and then stood, carrying her with him.

"Where are we going?"

"To bed, darling, where we can make love in warmth and comfort, where we can fall asleep together and then wake up and make love again."

She heard his words, felt their impact, her mind painting a picture of the two of them in her bedroom, undressing, lying on her bed, making love. That was replaced by a picture she had forgotten, one dragged out of the bottom of her memory, and she froze up, seeing her father and a strange woman in her parents' room while her mother lay dying in the hospital.

"Rick."

He stopped, something in her flat tone bringing

him to a halt. Slowly, he set her down on the second step of the stairs leading up to the front porch. Still holding her, he looked directly into her eyes. "What's wrong?" There was no censure in his voice, just loving care, deep kindness, and she wanted to weep for what she had to do.

"I can't. Not with my kids in there." She touched his rough jaw, feeling the whiskers that had so recently and so thrillingly abraded her softness. "I . . . I've never done anything like this. I can't. I want to raise them to be—does it sound stupid and old-fashioned to say 'good girls'? So I have to set an example for them, Rick. I'm sorry. I had no right to let things go so far out there."

He took her face into his big hands, turning it up to his. "Hey, we were both out there, you know. I'm even more responsible for what happened than you. I didn't give you much of a chance to make a decision, did I? And I respect what you're saying about your kids and the way you want to raise them. I love you for that. But come home with me, Sandy. Come to my bed."

She backed up to the third step. "No! I couldn't leave the girls at night, Rick. What if they needed me and I wasn't home? I never leave them alone at night. What if the house burned down?"

He laughed softly and hauled her back into his arms, burying his face in her hair. "You think of the most unlikely disasters," he said. "All right, then, I'll wait, but not forever. If I have to force the issue, I will."

"Rick—"

"Shhh. No." He laid a finger over her lips. "We'll talk another day. Mom's coming tomorrow with Roger. She'll stay a week or two. After that you and I are going to talk. Okay?"

"I don't know."

"That's all right," he said confidently. "You don't have to know. I do." And then, with another kiss that left her weak, he was gone.

Sandy crawled into bed, and lay there, feeling as if she had just played he loves me, he loves me not on a hundred daisies and come out a winner every time. Yet knowing what she did, feeling as she did, she shouldn't have been so happy in the knowledge of Rick's love. It was wrong. It was useless. And it was the most wondrous thing that had ever happened to her, and she held the knowledge closely as she slept.

Jane Gearing was indeed flamboyant. She greeted Sandy and the girls on the deck where Rick was barbecuing dinner. She was wearing an open, floor-length, tiger-striped robe that looked straight out of Africa; under that she wore skinny black pants with silver buttons from ankle to knee and a white silk blouse with the top three buttons undone. She had on heels that put her head on a level with Rick's, and Sandy caught herself staring in amazement, first at Jane, then at Rick, and then at Roger.

If she said anything, she wasn't aware of it, but she must have been functioning, because no one said anything odd to her. She sat down in a big wicker chair, her head spinning. Rick's mother *was* smoking a cigar, a cigar long and slim like Jane herself, and she gestured with it with elegance that Sandy could only admire in awe. But what awed her most was the striking resemblance between Jane and little Roger and a complete outsider—*herself*.

All that was his father in the child seemed to be concentrated in his huge, startlingly blue eyes that laughed and danced behind thick black lashes. Roger was so beautiful and so sweet that Sandy melted and fell in love with him within the space of two minutes. How could his mother ever have given him up?

His grandmother's strong genetic influence had provided Roger with a triangular face along with the dark hair and arched brows that gave them both a perpetually eager look. Jane's impish smile was echoed, flickering on and off Roger's face as he made shy advances to Sandy's children.

But Jane's eyes and Sandy's could have come from the same gene pool. Jane's hair was as long and as dark as Sandy's. It hung down her slim back in a glistening curtain that was shot through with silver streaks she flaunted rather than hid. With the exception of her greater height, she and Sandy had the same body type, and the resemblance was uncanny. They could have been mother and daughter.

Rick came up behind her and touched her shoulder with the cold side of a glass. She swung her gaze to his face, knowing he must see her amazement. Handing her the drink, he sang softly, " 'I want a girl, just like the girl.' You see it, don't you?"

But before she could answer, Jane was there, sitting beside her, probing with swift and charming questions until Sandy felt she had been thoroughly examined—and just as thoroughly approved. It left her feeling weak and stunned and totally bemused . . . and also incredibly good about herself.

For the next ten days Jane kept everyone's life in constant uproar. She teased the girls, making them howl with laughter; she teased Roger, snatching his thumb out of his mouth but making his big, dark-fringed eyes brim with mirth. She adored Sandy's house and declared that forthwith, decorating with picture postcards would be the "done" thing. She taught Never three new words, luckily in Chinese. Rick refused to tell even Sandy what they meant, saying only that he hoped they never got any neighbors who spoke Cantonese.

Jane played in the fountain as rowdily as any of the children; she climbed like a sleek cat to the very top and splashed all the way down, carrying Roger and leading the girls in a wet, noisy game of tag that she invited everyone else to join in.

She swiftly and efficiently rearranged Rick's

house, lambasting him cheerfully for his unimaginative placement of furnishings and paintings. "Just shoved against the walls the way the movers left things isn't good enough," she said. "No sense of adventure, or one of harmony. Terrible."

She hired a housekeeper named Mrs. Long, who was the epitome of sweet-faced, soft-spoken, white-haired grandmothers, and given to wearing house-dresses. She hired her, not for those reasons, but because Mrs. Long, during her first meeting with Roger said with a hint of steel in her voice, "I suggest you don't do that, Mrs. Gearing. I've raised four children and have eleven grandchildren. That thumb will come out when it's ready. Meantime, the child needs it."

From that day on, Jane stopped snatching Roger's thumb out of his mouth, and she knew she could safely leave him with a woman who was willing to stand up for his rights, even to his own grandmother.

And then she was gone, and the void she left behind was so great Sandy wondered if it would ever be filled, for not only had Jane gone, but Jenny and Pam, as well, on the way to visit their grandparents.

She sat on the deck at Rick's house, Roger playing quietly beside her. Jane had forbidden her to go to the airport with them, saying, "No way! You'd just cry. Ricky's taking me, and he can take them, too, since our flights are only an hour apart. You can stay here and do your blubbering in private. Look at those kids, darling, so proud of themselves, their first plane trip alone. Don't spoil it for them. Heavens, girl, you're raising them to be fine, independent women and they're nearly nine years old, so don't mess things up by dripping all over them at the airport."

Sandy had allowed herself to be bullied, but in fact she knew Jane was right; her tearful presence at the airport would detract from the girls' sense of great adventure, so she had done her blubbering and dripping in the privacy of Rick's bathroom and then come out on the deck to be with Roger. He got up from his play and came to lean on her knees. She rubbed a hand over his warm, soft hair. He had his thumb in his mouth.

"Sammy?" he said around it.

"Yes, Roge?" She smiled down at him, her heart twisting. He was such a love of a child.

"C'hi-hi-o-er-ap?"

"Anytime, sweetheart. My lap is at your disposal." She lifted him up and he nestled against her. Her lap had become one of his favorite resting places in the past couple of weeks.

"Rock?" he asked, and Sandy rocked, folding him close in her arms. He closed his dark lashes over his incredibly blue eyes. "Hing?" he asked around his thumb, and she sang. Presently, she realized he had fallen asleep, but still she sat there singing softly, one foot pushing the big, padded swing. It creaked, making a lullaby all its own.

That's how Rick found them. He stood at the edge of the deck and just looked at them in the twilight, two dark heads close together, two pairs of eyes closed sleepily. He felt his heart fill at the sight of them. He stepped closer, and Sandy's eyes opened, gazed into his for a long moment, and then flooded with tears. She blinked and two of them trickled down.

He crouched before her. "Don't, Sandy. They'll be all right."

"I know. And it's not that. Or not entirely. I'll miss them terribly, but . . . it's this!" She brushed her wet cheek against Roger's hair. "You play so dirty, Rick. You put this beautiful child into my life and I never wanted to love anyone again but my girls. Do you know what it does to me to hold him like this? Do you know what his need and his softness feel like to a mother whose children are growing up and away from babyhood? What his total trust in me does to my heart? He's still little more than a baby, Rick, and I never wanted any more babies to love until . . ."

"Until now?" he asked, smiling, stroking her hair and then Roger's, managing to touch her breast at the same time. She went completely still. During the time his mother had visited, he hadn't done anything to pressure her, hadn't pushed for any kind of a decision, hadn't even kissed her, and she had missed his caresses, his embraces.

"Until you met me, met my son? And now that you know us, love us, you want more babies?"

"I don't want more babies!" she said in a high, agitated whisper, "I can't *have* more! And I don't love you." Roger stirred against her and she rocked him quietly until he stilled, warm and heavy in her arms.

"Don't you?" Rick asked, getting to his feet and reaching for his son.

"No," she said sternly.

Rick carried Roger upstairs, Sandy tagging along, and together they slid him out of his clothes and into pajamas before tucking him in. Rick took Sandy's hand, leading her back down the stairs. She wanted to run but felt too numb. She wanted to hide but no corner offered itself. Rick wouldn't wait any longer. She knew that, and was still no closer to knowing what to do than she had been two weeks before.

They went outside and sat down on the swing. He didn't waste any time at all. "I want to marry you, Sandy."

Her breath left her lungs in a whooosh. She stared at him, bereft of words.

"Well?" he said lightly. "Doesn't a statement like that deserve some kind of reply? The least you could do is burst into tears and fling yourself into my arms. Or, if you don't like that one, how about a little blush and a mumbled 'Oh, but this is so sudden.' Or maybe you could try fainting so I could catch you."

"You've been reading too many romances."

"Well, honey, you have to make some sort of

response, have some kind of reaction." *Besides that terror-stricken look of yours,* he added silently.

"Rick, you've known from the beginning that I don't want to get . . ." Her voice faded away. "That I . . ." She shook her head and twisted her hands in her lap.

He took them and held them still. "Can't say it, Sandy? Can't force out the words? Why is that? Is it because you really do want to get married, to me?"

"I—no!" Panic struck her, and she tore her hands free, leaping to her feet, going to the rail and leaning on it, facing away. "No. It wouldn't work."

"Why not? We're compatible in every way, Sandy."

"You mean sexually." She turned as she said it and looked at him, not able to read his expression clearly in the dark. But of course that was what he meant. To a man, compatibility always meant sexual unity.

"Yes, I mean that. But I mean a lot more, too, and I think you know it. But for some reason, you're running scared." He strode across to her and pulled her tightly against his chest. "Don't be scared, love. Let me hold you. I will never hurt you."

You will, you will, a small voice inside her whimpered, but it was overridden by the surge of desire his kiss brought forth and she clung to his shoulders, feeling the hardness of his arousal pressing into her own softness. She wanted him so much, and gasped, arching, when he touched her breasts. It was just like the first time he had touched her. It wasn't supposed to be like the first time. Was every time with him going to be so thrilling, so fresh and new and exciting, like a journey just beginning?

"Make love to me," she whispered against his lips. "That other time, when I wouldn't let you come into my house with me because the girls were there . . . well, they aren't there now, Rick. Take me home. Love me like you said, in warmth and comfort, where we can fall asleep together and then wake up and make love again."

He stepped away from her, holding her hands still. "No."

She stared at him. "No?" She couldn't have heard him right.

"No," he repeated. "Thank you for the offer, Sandy. I love you and I want you, but not like that. If we go to your place to make love, how long will we go on doing that, hiding away, making a secret of it? For a day or two? A week? Until you get used to the idea that we are in love and are going to get married? Or only until your kids come home. And what happens then? Do we get married, or will I be banned from your bed again?"

She looked at him, tormented. "You make me sound so cold."

"That's the way your suggestion makes me feel."

"That's not the way it makes me feel," she cried, hurt and bewildered. "Thinking about making love with you makes me feel warm and good and achy all over. I want you. All your strength and power and . . . and everything. I want to feel you moving inside me. I want to sleep in your arms and wake up beside you and make love in the morning the way it happens in books. I've never made love in the morning, and I don't care what you say! Those aren't cold feelings!"

"No, darling. Of course they're not. They're warm and good and wonderful feelings and I share them with you. But I want to share more."

"It's the more that scares me," she said miserably. "The more that I know I don't have to give you. And when you demanded it of me, we'd start tearing at each other."

"No," he said, kissing her temple, moving his mouth down her face and flicking at the corner of her lips with the tip of his tongue, sending shivers of delight down her spine, but she pushed his face away.

"Don't," she said. "We have to talk. I have to make you see. How would you feel if you told me six times that you were bringing someone home for cocktails and dinner and when you arrived with your guest I was out in the garden building a rock wall with no dinner on the table and no ice in the freezer and up to my armpits in mortar?"

He hugged her tightly and rocked her from side to side. "Idiot. Why do you think we have Mrs. Long?"

She pushed away from him, shoving her hair out of her eyes. "And how would you feel if the school called and called because Roger was sick and they couldn't reach me because I was sitting on a stump somewhere on the far side of the valley designing landscaping for a new subdivision?"

"Again, why do you think we have Mrs. Long?"

"Then, dammit, why don't you marry Mrs. Long?" she shouted. She ran down the steps and headed for home. She slammed the gate behind her and locked it, taking the key with her. She continued to run full tilt down the path until she reached her rose arbor beside the stream. There she sat, huddling, weeping convulsively. "I don't want to get married! I don't want to get married!" She said it over and over as if someone were trying to force her. "I truly don't! Oh, heaven help me, what am I going to do?"

Six

At length, Sandy calmed herself and sat sniffing, watching the still silver of the pond, gazing out at the city lights below and the ghostly cone of Mount Hood. Then, turning her gaze toward the darkness of the trees between her house and Rick's, she whispered, "And I didn't want to fall in love with you either, but I did that."

In the darkness, a small, flickering light gleamed, bobbing up and down, and she stared at it until it blurred, starlike, before her eyes. What could it be? Whatever it was, it was coming nearer, and she realized it was floating down the stream. As that realization came, it bobbed over the little spillway under the bridge and came to a stop, swirling on the faint current of the pond, an arm's length out of reach. Sandy waded into the cool, muddy water.

It was a candle standing in a sardine can, and fixed tightly to it with a rubber band was a folded note. Still standing thigh-deep in water, she opened it and read it in the flickering light of the candle:

Because I don't think Mrs. Long could ever turn me on the way you do. Now, go to bed, my love. Don't sit out in that arbor all night. We'll work it out, Sandy. You'll see.

It bore no salutation, had no signature, but she recognized it as her first ever love letter. She clutched it to her breast as she waded out of the pond. Inside the house, she read it again and then tucked it into the box with her other precious mementoes. In the morning she arose at dawn and put her reply under his windshield wiper.

A man with X-ray vision can't be all bad, but you simply don't know what you'd be getting into. I love you, damn you, you omniscient, provoking man. However, you're wrong in this.

She didn't hear from him all that day, and though she sat by the pond all evening and half into the night, no more candles came floating downstream. Had he found it? He must have. So why the silence?

It wasn't until the following day when she got home late in the afternoon that she found her reply. It was in the form of a long, flat box leaning on her back door. With shaking hands she carried it inside and untied the strings. Opening the lid, she swept aside layers and layers of tissue paper and then held up the contents of the box, tears running down her face.

It was a floor-length dress of cream-colored silk with a lace overskirt dotted with tiny satin bows, each bearing a small pearl in the center. The sleeves were puffed and would come to her elbows and the neck was cut into a low scoop that would show off the string of pearls she found in a small box at the bottom of the larger one.

There was no note. None was needed. This was his reply. Walking carefully, as if something might break if she stepped too hard, Sandy carried the wedding dress into her bedroom and hung it as far back in her closet as she could reach. The pearls she tucked into her top drawer. She wouldn't be wearing them or the dress, and unless she did, she knew Rick wouldn't be back. Somehow, she would have to stop missing him.

Work would be her solace. Work would fill the gaps.

Leadenly, Sandy surveyed the lattice built by the carpenter who had long since moved on to another job. In the fullness of time, the seventeen feet of criss-crossed slats would be covered with sweet-scented honeysuckle, providing a screen for one side of the private garden she was creating outside the master bedroom of what she tried hard to think of as "the Gearing place." As she had known he would, Rick had backed off as a result of her silence. He hadn't tried to contact her since sending her the dress more than a week before. Luckily, his Landscaping by Aabab sign had borne fruit, and she had two more contracts to work on. She'd been scheduling her time at his house carefully, coming only when she knew he would be at work. And now the job was all but done, her last piece of work for him, and she was loath to finish.

It was a shady little garden with filtered sun behind the lattice, perfect for the lush moss that grew naturally on the rocks of the bluff, for the ferns that bowed gracefully toward the water of the pool. The splash of the waterfall was musical and kept the air humid; the shade, too, was perfect for the riot of colors made by tuberose begonias, impatiens, and coleus, planted in the five tiered beds of stone and mortar that she had built herself, starting near the top of the waterfall and tumbling down beside it.

A white wrought-iron bench stood near the pool, and backing the water was a stand of pyracantha—firethorn—covered now with frothy white blossoms which in winter would be replaced by brilliant scarlet berries, a lovely contrast to the blue spruce hedge that provided the other privacy screen.

Beside the stream, with a crushed shell path leading through it, and abutting the lattice, was a moongate, a perfect circle through which a person entering the garden from the outside had to pass. Evil spirits, she knew, could not pass through a circle, and somehow it was comforting to think that none would ever enter here.

Through that gate now stepped one of the world's least evil spirits.

He had his thumb in his mouth. Taking it out long enough to say, "Hi, Sammy," he immediately put it back in again, indicating that he wasn't truly happy. It amused and delighted Sandy that even without his thumb to garble his words, he still called her "Sammy." No one else did, and it was very special.

"Hi, Roge," she said, crouching and drawing him into the circle of her arms. "What's up?"

"I want to go see my mommy."

"Oh, love," she whispered, and scooped him up, going to the white bench. "Will I do, just for now?"

She sat down and held him close, rocking him, knowing she shouldn't be doing this, that there was no future in it, that she might be setting him up for even greater hurt later but unable to deny him the solace he needed. Was there some kind of a law that said she couldn't love him even if she never married his father?

For a long, precious time, he rested against her

and then raised his head, looking up at her trust-
ingly, his blue eyes shadowed. "Don't you and my
daddy like each other anymore?"

She swallowed hard. "Sure, honey. Of course
we do."

"But you don't come here anymore unless you're
working."

"I have an awful lot of work to do at other
houses, Roger," she told him, her heart aching.

"Will you sing?"

She tried, but after a few bars her voice refused
to cooperate. There were too many tears in her
throat. "I'm sorry, Roger. I guess I just don't feel
like singing today."

"But you were whistling when I got here. I like
it when you whistle, Sammy. It makes me feel
happy."

Had she been whistling? She hadn't been aware
of it. Did people whistle when they were dying
inside?

"Do you know how to whistle, Roge?"

"I'm not allowed to whistle."

She stared at him. "Who says? Why not?"

"It's too noisy."

Elaine's decree, obviously, not Mrs. Long's or
Rick's, Sandy realized. Neither objected to normal, happy sounds of childhood.

"I think you're allowed to now," she said. "Why
don't you try?"

His dark brows puckered the white skin of his

forehead. Unlike his father, Roger did not tan well. "Really? Daddy wouldn't get mad?"

Anger shook her. "Of course Daddy wouldn't get mad! He'd be so proud of you if you learned how to whistle. But you know what, hon?"

"Wha?" He had his thumb in place again.

"You can't whistle with your thumb in your mouth. Watch." Sandy pursed her lips and gave a sharp whistle, then put her thumb into her mouth and blew around it. Roger giggled.

Taking his thumb out of his mouth, he pursed his lips and made an ineffectual blowing sound. He scowled. "I guess I forgot how. I couldn't whistle very good."

Sandy smiled and tapped him on the nose. "I guess you're just going to have to learn how again."

"Prob'ly I can't."

"Prob'ly you can. Perserverance, Roger. That's what it takes."

His eyes widened. He loved big words. "What does that mean?"

"It means trying and trying and trying until you get there. Can you say it?"

"Perseverance," said another voice. "A word worth remembering."

Sandy set Roger on his feet and stood herself, holding him in front of her like a shield, behind her crossed hands. Eyes like pieces of the sky, filled with longing, held hers, and she could not look away. Still impaling her with his stare, Rick said, "Son, will you do something for me?"

"Sure, Daddy. I'm gonna learn how to whistle again. Sammy says I'm 'lowed."

"Sure you are. But right now I want you to go and tell Mrs. Long that I said it's time you . . . you learned how to . . . how to peel carrots."

Roger's eyes widened with the enormity of the privilege so unexpectedly granted. "Oh, boy! Okay, Dad."

He was scarcely out of sight before Sandy and Rick were crushed together, arms entwining, mouths clinging, both half sobbing with the intensity of their emotions.

"How I've missed you!" he moaned into the crook of her neck. "I've ached to feel you like this, so warm and alive and soft in my arms. I've been going out of my mind, wanting you. I give in, Sandy. I won't push for marriage, not right away. I need to love you."

"Me too, me too," she cried. "Hold me. Don't let me go. I love you so much, Rick."

"I won't let you go," he promised, lifting her and carrying her through a pair of golden curtains into his bedroom. He closed and locked the glass door. "Just you try to get away."

She didn't, and he locked the other door before laying her down on the bed, unfastening her hair from its workaday braid and twist to spread it out over the pillow, running his hands through it, sifting it, letting it fall in deep waves over her shoulders and breasts. His lips trembled as he kissed her mouth, then her eyelids, her neck.

"I'm dirty," she protested. "I have my sneakers on."

"Not for long," he said with a low, joyous laugh. "You won't have anything on for long." His hands seemed to be everywhere, sliding down over her aching breasts, hot through the fabric of her workshirt, stroking down over her thighs as he pulled them apart, placing one hand between them, his palm curving with insinuating weight that brought her arching up to him.

"This is where I've wanted you since the first time I saw you," he said, kneeling on the floor by the bed, slowly unbuttoning her shirt, unhooking her bra, bending to kiss the exposed skin. He freed her breasts, smiling at her involuntary gasp as he lifted them from below, gazing down on them as if they were treasures. His lips worked softly at her nipples, bringing them to hard peaks, and then sucking each one of them deep into his mouth as his fingers slipped down to open her jeans.

She raised her hips at his whispered urging and he tugged her jeans off, throwing them aside as he kissed her flat stomach, her thighs, his breath a burning stream of sensation moving closer and closer to her melting core of need. But when he tugged at her pink bikini panties, she stopped him.

She gasped. "No." At his wordless exclamation of shocked disbelief, she made a sound that was half laugh, half sob. "I mean, yes! Oh, yes, love, but I'm so dirty! Please, I want to come to you clean and sweet. Let me shower."

He laughed low in his throat as he got to his feet, lifting her and then standing before her, holding her away as he looked his fill. Then, smiling quizzically, he said, "What's this? Are you blushing? Sandy!" He swept her hair off her face and she squeezed her eyes shut in embarrassment.

"Darling, look at me," he said tenderly. Reluctantly, she opened her eyes.

His gaze was soft and loving and filled with dancing lights. The angled planes of his cheekbones were highlighted by the soft glow coming through the drapes, and his lips were curved into a smile. "I don't believe this. You're shy." He touched the warm underside of her breasts with both hands, lifting them so the hard nipples jutted upward.

"Don't," she said, hiding behind her hair again. "I'm not very good at this. I'm not used to standing around naked in front of a man." She felt like a fool, awkward and gawky and about as experienced as she'd been at nineteen. He wasn't holding her. There was nothing to stop her from walking across the room to the bathroom door—nothing except that she couldn't move. She crossed her arms over herself, hiding her breasts.

Rick nodded, his eyes on her face, and calmly shed his suit coat, pulled off his tie, and unbuttoned his shirt. He flung it away and took off his shoes and socks with the same unconscious grace he'd shown that day he'd stripped to his underwear in front of her, not twenty feet from where they now stood. Then, as he had that other day, he whipped his pants off, only this time, took his briefs with them and stood before her, nude, fully aroused, chest rising and falling steadily, quickly, flat abdominal planes taut, thighs apart and quivering as he watched her watching him.

Her hands fell from her breasts to hang loosely at her sides as she looked at him, wondering how any human being could be so perfect, so beautiful. He was unsmiling, watchful, waiting. Waiting for her. Waiting for her to trust him enough.

Slowly, she took a half step forward, lifted a hand and touched his chest, fingers trailing through the hair. She felt him tremble when she touched a nipple. Held by his gaze, compelled by it, she lifted her other hand to him. Now his mouth curved into a smile that tugged at her heart.

"I love you," he said. "You are very, very beautiful, Sandy. I want to touch you again."

She nodded, and his hands cupped her breasts, thumbs stroking over her nipples as her hands skimmed over his chest, splayed out flat as her whole body thrummed in response to his caresses, and in response to his response to her caresses. Lower and lower her hands trailed and she watched in something like awe as her fingers touched the hard velvet smoothness of his shaft, saw and felt it jerk involuntarily, and swung her gaze to his face, snatching her hands away, sure she must have hurt him.

"It's all right," he said, then gasped and thrust himself back into her hands. "I love it when you do that. Don't stop, Sandy, I . . . oh, yes, no, stop!"

He dragged himself out of her reach and lifted her, carrying her to the bathroom and, still holding her, managed to turn on the water and adjust it. Together they stood in the stinging spray, stroking, touching, smoothing soap over each other until Sandy was certain her legs would give way. Then, rinsing her, he sat her on the edge of the tub and knelt before her, kissing her breasts, her stomach, her feet and her knees. His lips and tongue caressed the insides of her thighs and then, as she went rigid with shock and pleasure, he thrust with his tongue against the aching, throbbing point and worked it until she cried out and dug her fingers into his back, convulsing again and again.

Dripping, he carried her limp body from the steam of the bathroom, overcome by urgency that could be denied no longer. He fought for control as he placed her on his bed, enfolded her with his arms and legs and covered her mouth with his own. He heard his breath coming harsh and rasping, struggled to steady it, but it burst from his straining lungs, sucked back in again, capturing her breath with it until he was filled with the essence of her, drowning in it, dying of it, over-flowing with the joy of being with Sandy at last.

Even as he told himself to slow down, to ease off, not to frighten her with the intensity of his need, her own hunger was returning and she moved against him, touching him, pulling him to her, parting her legs to welcome him into the haven of her body. He felt her lift to meet him, heard her soft, triumphant cry as they were joined, and felt her warm silk wrap around him, muscles contracting, squeezing him tightly, drawing from him all that he could give. Their fiery rhythms met, complemented, matched until they were on a high, stormy plateau together.

As they stared into each other's eyes, riding out the storm, wanting it never to end, both bodies convulsed massively into a vibrating rigidity that held for a long time before it released them to subside into each other's arms, blind, sweat-slicked, sated.

He tasted tears on her face and lifted his head to look at her. She was smiling. "I didn't know it could be like that. Oh, Rick, will it be like that again?"

He could have wept, too, feeling her tight flesh squeezing around him as her body pulsed in aftershocks.

"It'll be like that again sooner than you think," he said huskily, cupping her bottom as he rolled her on top of him. "I thought I knew myself, knew what I was capable of, but you've taught me different, love. It was never like this for me before either."

She read the truth in his eyes, felt the throbbing of his strength inside her, and squeezed with muscles she hadn't known she possessed, hadn't known she could control, drinking in his musky male scent as he clasped her hips and rotated her gently on him.

They made love slowly and sweetly this time, exploring not only each other's bodies but each other's responses, each other's tolerances for this stimulation, or that, and they laughed together, happy, learning so much, and loving what they learned, until the world turned rosy and tilted over to spill them into sleep.

A long time later Sandy awoke to know that he had covered them and that it was dusk outside the golden drapes. Rick was awake, watching her. He kissed her and then spoke.

"Whatever it is we've found, sweetheart, we can't let it go. We can't let each other go. You have to see that, Sandy. You must!"

He saw confusion and pain in her eyes as she covered his lips with a finger, preventing him from going on. He drew her finger inside his mouth, watching her eyes darken into luminous pools, shimmering with desire before he released her again.

"When I got your note, I thought the world had just been handed to me whole," he said. "To have you admit that you loved me was the most wonderful feeling. I can't describe what I felt. I went to your house but you'd already left for work. I thought about going in search of you, but decided against it. Then, when I got home the next night, it was late. I went down to the gate and found it locked. I was going to send you another candle, but the wind blew out my last match. I headed up here for more, but then I looked at that bent black wick and I decided not to light it. It wasn't the right kind of candle. I want an everlasting one, Sandy, one that will burn for us as long as we live. And I want it lit by you too."

Tortured, her voice thick with tears she didn't want to shed, she asked, "But what if I don't have that kind of candle, Rick?"

"You do," he responded. "You just have to find it, love. It's inside here." He tapped her chest. "I know it's there."

"Will you . . . will you help me find it?"

"I'll help you every day for the rest of our lives. This love we share isn't going to die, Sandy. It's only going to get bigger and better and stronger. We will grow together."

"We'll grow. I know that. But what if we grow, change, at different rates? There are so many broken marriages, and bad ones that are held together for the sake of the children. We have three children between us, Rick, who would be devastated if our marriage failed."

"There's no reason why it should."

"Isn't that what you thought when you married

Elaine? Didn't you love her, have high hopes for the future together?"

He sat up and leaned against the headboard, frowning. "All right. Yes. But I wasn't the man then that I am now. Now I would never marry a woman like Elaine. She was weak. She hated making decisions. She looked up to me, I guess, and relied on me to do everything. And while it was a real ego booster at first, it palled. It grew old very fast. I knew quite soon that I wanted an equal in marriage, not a little girl who needed me to look after her as if I were her daddy. I wanted a woman, Sandy, a complete, mature adult partner. I wanted someone like you. And now that I've found you, I want you to be my partner in marriage."

"Even though I'm going to have to work long hours every day of the week for the next fifteen years or however long it takes to pay off my debts?"

"We could work together to do that, love."

"No!" Her voice was sharp. "I won't let you do that, Rick. I'd rather come to you free and clear, but I don't think I can wait that long either. I—"

He dragged her up against him, his eyes blazing. "Am I hearing you right? Are you saying you'll marry me? Now?" He leaned his head back and laughed as he cradled her, straining her to him. "You will?"

"I will."

"Oh, love. Love. Why do I feel like crying?"

She laughed, too, and snuggled close. "I don't know, but please, don't. Just hold me. Tight."

"Forever, Sandy. Oh, sweetheart, don't be afraid," he said, holding her as tightly as she'd asked, feeling her trembling, and knowing she was on the verge of panic again. "I won't let anything happen to us." Then, hearing what he'd said, he amended it. "*We* won't let anything happen to us. Together we'll make it work."

Inside, a little voice nagged at her, *But what if we don't?* She ignored it as Rick slowly began touching her body again, and she his, as they reaffirmed their love, the greatness of it, the goodness, and the power.

Then, much later, when she arose and began to dress, he flicked on a bedside lamp, looked at her, and said, "Don't go. Stay with me, love. All night. Every night."

"I can't. I didn't want you to sleep with me when my children were in the house, so how could I act differently with your child in the house? It's the same thing, Rick. Exactly the same. This is Roger's home, and before you say that you want to spend what's left of the night in my bed, let me remind you that your son expects you to be here in the morning."

He hitched himself up and grinned at her before getting out of bed and pulling on a pair of jeans. "I hope you won't insist on separate beds—or worse, separate rooms—when we're married."

She shook her head, feeling stupidly shy again as she hooked up her bra while he watched. Just the thought of being married to him, of waking up every morning with him, was enough to rock her back on her heels. A shudder of delighted anticipation raced through her as she buttoned her shirt.

"You don't have to come with me," she said when he opened the sliding door to go outside.

"Oh, yes, I do," he said sternly, putting an arm around her. "You are very precious to me, my love."

She leaned her head on his shoulder for a moment. She had never been precious to anyone before in her life. She thought she could get to like it. But not too much, she reminded herself quickly, remembering what he'd said about Elaine. Not that there was a lot of danger of her becoming anything like that. She would never be a clingy wife anymore than she would ever be a milk-and-cookies mom.

"All right," she said, "but just as far as the gate."

"Lock it," he said. "And take the key with you, or you might find me slipping under the covers beside you in an hour or so."

She smiled and touched his cheek. "I wouldn't fight back if you tried it."

"No, but you'd kick me out before dawn, wouldn't you?"

She nodded, feeling sad and scared again. "I'd have to. Candle flames show only in the dark."

"Not ours, Sandy." he said with supreme confidence. "Ours shines big. It shines bright. Or it will, when we've both lighted it." He kissed her quickly and thrust her through the gate. "Good night, my darling. Remember that I love you."

She carried that thought with her into sleep, only to find herself abruptly awake again, sitting erect, eyes wide, sheet drawn up around her naked form, staring with unreasoning terror into the dark, waiting for—what?—to happen again.

Seven

A rattling came at her window, then a hoarse, croaking call. Never? Was he hurt? Was something after him? She leapt from her bed, snatching up her robe and thrusting her arms into the sleeves, fumbling for the belt, only to drop it again as she went stiff with terror. *Smoke!* She smelled smoke, heard an ominous crackling.

Fire! Her first, instinctive reaction was *the kids!* before she recalled that they weren't there. She flew to the door, remembering just in time to feel it before opening. It was scorching hot to her hand and she whirled. The window! Escape! Without further thought she shoved it open and straddled the sill, then hesitated.

Her box, her box of precious things. She had to

have that. Everything in it was irreplaceable—baby pictures, important papers . . .

"My love letter!" She lunged for the closet, tore open the door, and snatched at the box. It was jammed. She pulled harder and it came loose abruptly, overbalancing her, and she fell to the floor between the bed and the window just as the door burst inward on a blast of superheated air that seared her face as she struggled up. She smelled the horrible odor of burning hair as she choked and clawed her way back to the window, shoving the box before her, turning as she crawled to look over her shoulder at the deep well of pulsating, roaring fire behind her. Outside, she staggered to her feet, beat out small flames licking at the hem of her robe, grabbed up the box, and ran for the office. The door was locked. *Of course it is,* she told herself. *It's nighttime!* With a rock she broke a window, hearing the tinkling glass as a counterpoint to the deep roar of the fire, feeling the awesome heat roll toward her. The telephone was a solid, comfortingly real object in her hand, but her frenzied mind refused to give up the emergency. She dialed O.

How could a voice be so serene in the middle of an obscene maelstrom? How could the woman simply say "Operator," as if flames and sparks were not lighting up the night with the power of a million candles?

"My house is on fire!" she screamed into the phone, and somehow, in response to the operator's calm tones, managed to say where the emergency was located.

"All right, they're on their way," said the operator. "You'll hear the sirens soon. Is everyone out of the house?"

Numbly, Sandy answered the questions put to her, knowing on one level that the other woman was deliberately keeping her on the line, and calm, so that she wouldn't do something stupid. When she heard the sirens, she hung up and went out to open the gates.

As she swung them wide, Abe came running, his eyes staring, his bushy brows high, his meager hair sticking straight up. He took one side of the heavy gates and then came to her, hugging her without words as the first of the fire engines came screaming in, heeling over as they made the turn with little reduction in speed.

Within the fiery furnace that had once been a home, seven hundred and fourteen postcards, souvenirs from around the world, covering one woman's seven decades, were burning. Framed newspaper pictures of a granddaughter known only through that medium were destroyed in flares of heat. Sandy, at five, being rescued from the topmost branches of a tree by a smiling fireman on a ladder. Sandy, at eleven, industriously puffing her cheeks out as she played a tuba nearly as big as she in her school's marching band. Sandy, at twenty, big-eyed and scared, trying hard to look happy in her wedding gown beside a trapped-looking Alex. And then no pictures, just a tiny classified ad, yet carefully clipped and mounted behind glass like all the others. *To Sandra (née Aabab) and Alex Filmore, twin daughters, Jennifer and Pamela.*

And on the porch rail, completely engulfed even as the streams of water gushed over it, a small bonsai oak flared and burned, and Sandy cried aloud in pain that was not entirely hers, but Abe's and her grandmother's and, maybe, even her father's, because, through his own doing, he had missed so much, lost so much.

His mother, though, had done what she could.

Burning there were fifty-some years of memories of a renegade, unforgiving son who had left at the age of sixteen, and never returned, never kept in touch, denying his mother the right to know her only grandchild, her daughter-in-law whom she might have loved as the daughter she had never had.

Forty years of varnish, layer upon layer, forty years of paint, the variety of colors showing in chipped spots here and there. Forty years of wallpaper, of floor wax, of furniture polish—ignited, roaring, crying out in the pain of a violent death.

Sandy looked into Abe's old face, seeing in his eyes the anguish of watching precious reminders of a lifelong love destroyed. He gave her a slow smile, and shook his head. His memories, she knew, would live on in spite of the loss.

A hoarse cry drew her out of Abe's hold, and

Sandy heard her name shouted again as the wildly careening figure of a man, his form impaled on the beam of a searchlight, tore out of the dark toward the burning house. Two firemen ran at him on converging courses, but he thrust them aside easily, sending them flying as he continued to streak toward the fire, screaming Sandy's name. She reached him before the two men could recover and flung herself into his path. She, too, would have been swept aside, but he tripped on her and together they went down, caught in the spray from the stream of a hose.

"Rick! Rick! No!" He fought her, demented, and she hit him in the throat, making him choke, and he stared at her, sanity returning, then scooped her up, running from the heat and the flames. On the far side of the pond, outside the little twin playhouses, he collapsed to the ground, still holding her. In the flickering light she could see blood streaming down the side of his face from a cut on his temple. He was weeping.

"I thought you were in there. I thought I had lost you. I saw the fire. I couldn't sleep and I saw the flames and I thought I'd never get here in time." He covered her face with kisses and tears and fire-hose water, smearing her soot onto him. He ran his hands into her long hair, holding her head to kiss her and then reeled back in horror, staring down at his hands.

They were filled with clumps of hair.

"Sandy, darling, you're burned," he said. "Your

face, your beautiful hair." He clutched her to him and she clung, trembling now with reaction, her muscles and bones aching. She wanted to hide. She wanted to sleep. She wanted Rick to hold her forever, but he was trying to put her from him.

"No, no. Sit up, love. Let me see. Let me get help. Sandy, let go! You're burned."

"No, I'm not. Just hold me. I'm so scared. I'm still so scared. It's all over but I can't stop shaking."

A fireman came then, following Abe, who handed Rick a blanket to wrap around Sandy. "She's hurt," said Rick in quick denial of Sandy's assurances that she was fine. "She's burned and in shock. Her face, her hair. Call an ambulance."

A flashlight played over her face before the official asked, "Are you burned?"

"No. Just singed. I'm fine, really."

"She looks okay," the man said soothingly to Rick, "but you're bleeding." Quickly, he sponged the cut and pressed a bandage over it. "How'd that happen? When the lady tackled you?"

"I had to climb over a ten-foot fence to get here. I fell."

"Any other damage?"

"I got up and ran the rest of the way, so I guess not. Now, do you call an ambulance for my fiancée or do I report you for negligence?"

"Rick!"

"It's okay, ma'am. He's just a bit—agitated. How about you let me have a better look at you and then we'll decide?"

To appease Rick she nodded, and the fire chief, well-trained in first aid, ran gentle fingers into her hairline, coming away with more burned fuzz. "Your skin hurt?"

She shook her head. "No worse then a sunburn," but when she tried to sit down again, she couldn't control the wince as her knees bent.

"What is it?" the two men snapped in concert.

"The backs of my legs sting a little," she admitted. "The room was . . . sort of hot as I went out the window."

Rick shuddered, his solid body close against hers, and the other man looked at her sharply. "I'll take a look at that, too, if you don't mind."

He suggested she see her doctor the next day if she felt it necessary, but pronounced the burns only superficial. "You got out just in time, didn't you?"

She must have looked guilty, because he narrowed his gaze at her and asked suspiciously, "Or did you go back inside?"

She shifted her gaze away from the wide beam of his light. "No . . . not exactly."

Rick pounced. "What does that mean?"

"It means I was almost out when I realized I didn't have my"—how could she say *baby pictures* and expect to have two men understand? —"insurance policies and other important . . . stuff," she quickly ad-libbed. "The bedroom door sort of puffed inward just as I was about to head back to the window. But I got out in plenty of time," she added quickly as Rick moaned.

With Abe beside them, they watched quietly as the firemen did their job. The stench was abominable and Sandy wanted to leave but somehow could not. There was nothing she could do, yet it seemed she should stay until the flames were finally doused and the hoses shut off. As Never fluttered, nattered, then became subdued to perch on Abe's bent knee, she decided it was a death watch and they were all in on it.

"He saved my life," Sandy said, stroking the big bird as she explained how Never had squawked and rapped on the window.

"I'm going to buy him a whole case of car keys," said Rick, then leapt to his feet and cursed as powerful lights flooded over them and a television camera whirred. Swiftly, he spoke to the news team and then dispatched them before returning to Sandy and Abe.

"Come on, let's go home. Abe, there's lots of room, and your house will smell of smoke almost as much as this area does."

Abe declined, as Sandy had known he would, and ambled slowly back to his little shack behind the greenhouses.

Mrs. Long was waiting for them on the front deck, fully dressed but with her white hair tied up in a net. Her face broke into lines of relief at the sight of them and then into amazement as Rick bent his arm and set a singed raven onto the rail.

"Oh, you poor child," said Mrs. Long to Sandy. "You come along with me, dear. What you need is a bath and something soothing to drink."

"Thank you, Mrs. Long," Rick said, half carrying Sandy inside. "I'll take care of her. You try to get some more sleep, okay? Roger will be awake in a couple of hours."

Sandy was beyond caring. She stood, shivering with shock as Rick took her precious box from her and set it on the vanity in the bathroom. He peeled her ruined robe from her, and then stripped himself to hold her in the warm spray of the shower. He shampooed her hair, watching as more clumps of it slid into the drain, clogging it so the water rose around their legs. He gently sponged her sooty face, then soaped and rinsed her body until she was pink all over again before lifting her out and wrapping her in a big towel while he blow-dried her hair.

Moments later he tucked her into his bed and slid in beside her, holding her close, his hands making long, strong stroking motions down her back, trying to ease some of the trembling tautness.

Even with her eyes open she could see the flames and hear the roar. It was dawn and the golden light pouring through the curtains, bouncing off the moving water outside, held a terrible likeness to the horror she had witnessed. Only the touch of his body against hers held madness at bay. Only his arms and his skin and his scent, the steady sound of his heartbeat, kept terror from springing forth in resounding screams.

When her trembling had subsided to only an occasional shudder, he thought she slept, but she lifted her head and looked down at him. "I love you. Thank you for being here for me."

"Oh, sweetheart, don't ever thank me for doing what I want to do most in the world—look after you, care for you, keep you safe."

"Make love to me," she whispered, moving against him. "Fill me with yourself, Rick. Make me complete."

"You should sleep," he murmured, but his protest was weak, and she felt him shudder as her hands moved over his chest to his back. His lips met hers then, and she opened her mouth, drawing him into her warmth as he hardened and thrust deeper, then moved down her body, kissing away her tension, replacing it with another kind until the erotic plunge and intimate stroking of his tongue made her moan and surge up to him, needing the solace of his love.

He gave her what she needed and she cried out, arching into a quivering bow as he entered her, moving with her, holding her tightly as she tumbled, twisted, buffeted on turbulent currents far from earth, Rick her only reality, capturing her with his magic until she convulsed again and again and then tumbled back to earth in his arms.

"I love you," she whispered. "Oh, how I love you." For long moments she let her hands rove over his skin, feeling the hard muscles of his shoulders and arms and back, the sensitive, peaked nipples within their nest of silky hair on his chest, wetting them with her tongue until he growled softly. She loved his response, her own breath quickening as she drew in the musky scent of his desire, feeling it inflame her anew, and when she slid her seeking mouth downward, his body went rigid and a harsh, gasping sound was torn from him. *"Sandy!"*

She loved him as he had loved her, with lips and tongue and burning breath, his arching pleasure increasing her own until the two of them flew again and they shared a deep, shattering climax that seemed to go on and on before it released them. And then sleep came in deep black waves, carrying Sandy into a quiet place where the memories and dreams were only of good things.

When she awoke, the sun was high and Rick was sitting beside her fully dressed, waving a cup of coffee under her nose. Smiling, she sat up against the pillows he adjusted for her and greedily took the coffee.

"You are so beautiful," he said softly, loving her with his eyes. When her coffee cup was half empty, he set a tray on her lap, uncovering a dish of scrambled eggs and bacon with triangles of golden toast.

"Have you been up for long?"

"Long enough to have missed you unbearably," he said. "Now eat. I want to see all of that gone."

When she had eaten all she could, he kissed the toast crumbs from the corners of her mouth and took the tray off her lap. "The fire marshal will be down at the nursery at one o'clock," he said. When she glanced at her wrist—automatically and futilely, her watch having been on her bedside table—he added, "it's just after eleven. You go on into the bathroom and shower if you want. I'll be right back to help you."

But he had barely gotten out of the bedroom when a loud, anguished cry made him drop the tray and lunge back in, diving through the bathroom door to see her backed against a wall, face buried in her hands, rocking, keening, and he snatched her hands down, demanding, "Stop that! What's wrong?"

She looked up at him with drenched, tragic eyes and moaned, "You said I was beautiful. You lied!"

With a great, heaving sob of despair, she went on. "I don't have any eyebrows! I don't have any eyelashes! I look like a freak! I'm ugly! My hair is half an inch long and I don't have anything to *wear*!"

The enormity of her loss overcame her and she wailed against his chest, "I didn't save anything, Rick! My grandmother's things, her furniture, she polished it and cared for it and loved it for all those years and I let it burn up! And the tree. The little Gloria tree she grew especially for me. She looked after it for me for twenty-nine years be-

cause she never had a chance to give it to me, and
I could have grabbed it from the porch rail but I
forgot! How could I have forgotten my tree? And
the kids' bikes! We saved for so long and they were
only second hand but they loved them. My kids
have no home to come back to and no toys and no
clothes and I want to get dressed because I'm cold
and I don't have so much as a pair of panties and
I look like a . . . a . . . damned *amoeba*!"

Rick couldn't help it. He roared with laughter.
He'd thought there was something wrong. He
wrapped her in a towel and sat down on the bench
by the tub, rocking her on his lap. "You are beautiful," he assured her. "You're gorgeous, and you're
mine and I love you like crazy. Don't cry, sweetheart. You and your kids have a home and you
know it." He lifted her face, palming her tears
away, kissing her nose and then standing her on
her feet before rising as he said, "Or didn't you
plan on living with me after we're married?"

"I . . . yes. Of course. I wasn't thinking that far
ahead, I guess."

"That far?" he asked. "How far into the future
do you put our marriage? Not too far, I hope."

"No, not far, but . . . well, after the girls get
back. Rick? You didn't tell Roger, did you?" He
shook his head, wondering why she found the
idea so alarming, and she went on. "Good, we'll
tell all three of them together. Later, when the
girls are home. The girls . . ."

Her face crumpled again. "How can I tell them all their things are gone?"

"It'll be hard, honey, but I'll be right beside you to help, and don't forget, you did save this stuff, and what was lost was insured. It can be replaced." He opened her cardboard box, bending the flaps back, reaching in to find something, anything, to comfort her.

He drew out his hand, his face turning a ghastly gray, his voice dropping to a disbelieving croak as he held up the first item he'd found. "Your *insurance policies*? This is what you saved?" He flung a pair of pink terry sleepers at her. His voice rose to an outraged bellow as he plunged into the box again. "You risked your life for a dead man's *bathrobe*?" He flung that at her, too, and it clung to her left shoulder before slithering to the floor, carrying her towel with it.

He pounded with one fist on the vanity, making the box and his can of shaving gel bounce. His eyes glittered with a hard anger and his mouth was a thin white line in the gray of his face. He sucked in a harsh breath and thundered, "Well, to hell with you, lady! To hell with your *insurance policies*! They won't be needed on my behalf! You could have left the baby clothes to burn. I've had a vasectomy!

"And as for the bathrobe, you won't need it as protection against me! The woman I wanted as my wife has her priorities in order, knows what's important, and you obviously aren't the woman I thought you were. You can just take your precious insurance policies and . . . where the hell do you think you're going?"

Swiftly, he caught her, swinging her back into the bathroom. "You don't have any clothes on!"

"I don't have any clothes to put on!" she shouted. "Let go of me. I'm leaving. I don't have to stay here and listen to this! I took Alex's verbal abuse for five years and I won't take it any more from anyone. Ever! Now, get the hell out of my way. I'll live in a greenhouse before I'll stay here!"

"The hell you will! You'll stay here." His hands were tight on her shoulders. "You're in no shape to make any kind of decision. You'll do what you're told, woman!"

Sandy finally knew what the expression "to see red" meant. Through a fiery haze she stared at him. "I'll do what I'm *told*? Did I hear you say that? Do you think my having slept with you gives you the right to dictate to me? So I'm not the woman you thought I was, huh? Well, let me tell you, buster, you are exactly the kind of man I feared you were. Exactly the kind of man all men are—arrogant, bullying, dictatorial, a petty tyrant!" she finished on a furious shout, hands clenched, her jaw so tensed her teeth ached.

"I'll have to be a tyrant to counter the screaming shrew in you!" he roared, and when he slammed the bathroom door, the mirrors shuddered.

Shaking with rage, Sandy stood where she was,

moving only when a gentle knock sounded on the door and Mrs. Long asked if she could come in.

Snatching up Alex's robe, Sandy wrapped herself in it and opened the door to admit a carefully expressionless housekeeper who handed her two department store bags and then left in a big hurry.

Warily, she opened them as if they might contain snakes, but there was only clothing and toiletries.

Lacy pink matching panties and bra. Another set in blue, one in white. A red terry top with a square neck and broad straps over the shoulders to team with a pair of white shorts. There were sandals and they fit, and jeans which would also fit—but barely, and makeup in all the right shades.

It was the satin nightgown that made her pause, however, stroking the fabric, then balling it up and stuffing it deep into the bottom of the bag before stepping into the shower to scrub and scrub and scrub.

When she was dried, she discovered that the lacy pink underwear fit perfectly. Of course. She remembered his hands on her. He would know just how big she was everywhere. The jeans slid over her hips and clung with hardly any leeway at all, and the red top put a bit of color into her cheeks and a sparkle into her lashless eyes, but not even the bold red of the lipstick could hide the droop of her mouth.

She picked up her new hairbrush, but after a few strokes put it back down again, fresh tears of grief spilling over at the loss of her luxurious hair, hair that had been her one and only real vanity.

She dried her eyes and picked up the mascara, but of what use was mascara to a lashless woman?

With another self-pitying sniff she collected all her belongings and placed the bags on top of the box before stepping out into Rick's bedroom on stealthy feet.

He wasn't there, and she walked out through the sliding doors, through the private garden where the waterfall burbled into the pool, and through the circle of the moongate, heading for home, but even as she fled his house, she knew she had no home to flee to.

It was the loneliest feeling in the world.

Eight

Sandy was sitting in her mercifully untouched rose arbor, staring blindly at the placid ducks, when she heard Rick's footsteps in the gravel behind her. He came to stand before her, wearing white shorts, a blue T-shirt, and dark brown sandals. His hands were jammed into the pockets of his shorts, and he just stood there, looking at her, as if he didn't know what to say.

Neither did she, except for one thing.

"I'm sorry," she said softly, hopelessly.

"So am I," he said. "I didn't mean it."

She swallowed hard and blinked. "I did."

He sat beside her. "No. You didn't mean it, Sandy. You're hurt. I hurt you. I hammered on you when you were at your most vulnerable. But you still love me."

It was almost a question, but not quite.

She nodded. "Of course I do."

They both stared at the ducks, at the water. A hummingbird dive-bombed the fuchsia bush before probing into a ballerina-shaped flower, making it dance. The bird's bright red gorget flashed in the sun.

Sandy sighed. "Rick?"

"Yeah?"

"Remember that note you floated down to me?"

"Sure." He flicked a glance at her quickly, then away again.

"That . . . that was what decided me. Last night. To go back for the box. It was the only love letter I'd ever received and I couldn't let it burn. That, and the kids' baby pictures."

"Oh."

The silence went on, but the hurting didn't seem so intense.

"What did the fire inspector say?"

"Faulty wiring. The insurance man was here too."

"Mmm-hmm?"

"Too bad it wasn't the kids' playhouses that went up. There's about enough to replace them. Or an opulent doghouse." Her light laugh had a crack in it. They both stared at the ducks and the water some more.

Rick took her hand and held it palm-up on his sun-warmed thigh, bending her fingers inward one by one as if fascinated by the way they worked.

She wanted to crawl into his lap and howl out her pain.

"So?" He began to straighten her fingers, one by one. "What are you going to do now?"

"*Right* now?" Again, she laughed, a crackling sound that cut into his ears like a buzz saw. "I'm going to get my hair done." She got to her feet, taking her hand back.

He sat staring at her as if she were crazy.

"I can't think of anything more constructive to do."

He got to his feet, standing less than a foot from her. His pain was her pain. Her hand lifted all by itself and touched him. "It'll get better."

His hand covered hers, flattening it onto his chest, holding it as his gaze held hers. "All we did was have a fight, Sandy. I can't believe you're willing to snatch heaven out of my grasp just because we had a fight. Couples fight all the time. And make up. This can't mean the end of everything."

"It does. It has to. It was the end for me. Don't you remember what you said? That I'd do what I was told? You stood there handing down edicts regarding my behavior and actions. That was the kind of marriage my mother had, the kind I had, too, because I'd learned from the cradle that when a man spoke, a woman hopped, that when a man was mad a woman went around on tiptoe and did whatever he said. It took me a long time to un-learn those lessons and now I'm raising two daughters I want to be different. I thought you were different, that with you it would work, that you respected me. I thought the very notion of my bowing down and accepting you as some kind of superior being with the right to make all the rules was alien to you."

"Dammit, I don't want to make all the rules. I never said I did, but—"

"But?" she said goadingly when he broke off with a grimace. "But what? You're like ninety-nine point nine percent of all the men in the world, with the inborn conviction that having planted your flesh in mine, like an explorer planting a flagpole in the soil of an unknown island, you can say, 'Sorry, but your time of self-determination is over; your conqueror has arrived.' "

He scowled at her, then let out a gusty sigh that ruffled the front of her hair.

"See? You can't deny it. You think you own me now."

"I can't deny that I felt—at that moment—that I was better able to make decisions than you were. Dammit, you are the woman I love. And I was so furious with you for having done something so stupid it almost got you killed, I could have strangled you." He shook his head, chagrined. "I know. I know. Dumb."

"Dumb," she agreed. "But can you see now why all that changed my mind? It's not just you, Rick. I know myself. I know it would be pointless for me to marry you or any other man who thought he could dominate me like that."

He shook his head stubbornly. "No. I don't see it. Oh, sure, about you marrying any other man, yeah, but me? I mean . . . hell, a *flagpole*?"

He buried her spurt of laughter with his mouth, holding her against him. Her left hand stayed flattened on his chest between them, but her right, out of control, slipped down his back, over his buttocks, and came to rest at the top of his thigh. His body was hot against hers, the scent of him like home. *Just for a minute,* she told herself. *I'll stay just for a minute. I love him so much. I need him.*

She nestled her cheek just below his throat and felt his face on the crown of her head.

"I want you to give me a chance," he said. "All I ask is a chance to show you you can trust me. I won't push for an early wedding date. Not yet. I'll let you learn that with us it won't be the way you're afraid it will be. Please?" He cupped her face and turned it up to his, his expression pleading, tender, understanding, and sad all at the same time. Along with very, very determined.

Sandy nodded, feeling her eyes sting. "Okay. But, Rick, please don't hope too much. Maybe I'll never be able to give you that much trust." She felt like a fraud, because it wasn't his pleading she was giving in to, but that of her own aching heart which was fast overruling her sensible head.

"And now," he said, "you were going to have

something done about your hair?" She nodded and stepped back from him. He pulled his billfold out of his back pocket. "Honey, I know you can't have any cash, or even a checkbook, so—"

"No," she interrupted quickly. "I can filch cash from the float in the till and the bank will give me a new checkbook." She thought of asking for a bill for the things he had bought her this morning but decided he had to be allowed to give her something. She was almost certain that he'd never throw it up to her.

Anger flared for an instant in his eyes, but he fought it down and nodded. "Right. Do you need a ride into town?"

She shook her head. "What with Never's liking for keys, I've made a habit of keeping an extra set for every vehicle in the office safe."

He smiled. "My smart lady. Dinner's at six. See you."

A couple of hours later Sandy pulled her car to a halt in the circular drive at the front of Rick's house. With a shaking hand she tilted the mirror and looked at herself, still unable to believe that the image she saw was that of Sandy Aabab.

A cap of short dark curls fluffed saucily over her head and feathered the edges of her cheeks. Her flyaway, penciled-in brows added a touch of drama that was more than exotic, especially above the ridiculously long, thick lashes that now fanned from her upper eyelids. They were heavy and drew her lids down in a way she thought sinfully sexy and totally delicious. Blush on her cheeks, supplied by her very helpful hairdresser, made her brown eyes sparkle, and bright lipstick gave her mouth a moist look.

"I don't know why I didn't get my hair cut years ago," she murmured to the reflection in the narrow mirror before she twisted it back into position.

But, in fact, she did know, and thought about it as she got out of the car, pulling her new purse and several other purchases with her. She had kept it long because first her father, and then her husband, had made it clear that long hair was expected of a woman. Alex had gone so far as to forbid her to have it cut, and after the divorce, when she might have felt rebellious enough to do it, there had been no money for visits to the hairdresser. Besides, she was so used to having it long that had she thought about it, she probably would have believed she kept it that way by choice. Why, just this morning she'd been in tears over its loss. Only now that it was gone, she felt free and young and oddly excited.

Mrs. Long opened the door for her, with Rick right behind. He stared at Sandy, his jaw dropping, and swallowed convulsively. He took her hand and drew her into the foyer.

Then, speaking briskly, he turned to the housekeeper. "Mrs. Long, I want you to call a security company. Tell them we need a vault installed. It has to be . . . oh, about five foot three, all dimensions, with walls eight feet thick, and I want it buried deep in the cellar."

"We don't have a cellar, Daddy," said Roger, coming from the direction of the kitchen.

"They'll have to dig one."

"Sammy, you look pretty!" Roger ignored his father. "Your room is right next to mine. Pam and Jenny's is across the hall. Want me to show you?"

Sandy managed to tear her gaze from Rick's. Gratefully, she took Roger's hand. "Sure, Roge. I'd like that." His hand was warm and soft in hers, and yet it gave her the strength to walk past his father and mount the stairs.

Hers was a corner room at the front of the house overlooking the rolling green lawn and meandering stream she had built. Soft green curtains billowed in the gentle breeze, casting patterns of sunlight and shade across the cream carpet and jade-colored bedspread. She shared her adjoining bathroom with Roger. This was more opulence than she and the girls were used to. She felt a thrill of fear. What if she let her kids get accustomed to living like this and it didn't work out after all? Would they ever forgive her?

Of course they would, she told herself briskly as she followed Roger back downstairs for dinner. They were good kids, and material things weren't terribly important to them. Yet.

"Thanks, Mrs. Long," she said after dinner. "That was lovely. I'll do the dishes."

"You will not," said the housekeeper briskly. "Rick, take her out onto the deck. I'll bring coffee. No, don't argue and don't touch a single dish, young woman. You have enough jobs of your own to do without helping with the housework here."

Sandy smiled as she sat beside Rick in the big swing on the deck. "Doesn't she realize that I not only don't have any housework of my own to do, I don't have any house in which to do it? Not," she added, "that I'm complaining about lack of housework. If the house had to burn down, I'm glad it didn't happen right after I'd vacuumed, or something, or done a lot of cooking. As a matter of fact, the fire even cooked two beef roasts and one chicken right in the deep freeze. Neat, huh?"

"Sandy." Rick wasn't fooled by her attempt at lightness. "I'm sorry it's all lost."

She sighed and rested her head on his shoulder. "It's my own fault. I should have made sure I had a replacement policy. The trouble with the kind I bought is that by the time you take forty years depreciation off nearly everything, there's not much left. When I get my insurance check, I plan to take all of you out for dinner. At Burger King."

Rick hugged her tightly. "I said I wouldn't push, and truly, I'm not, but if you'd just marry me right now, you wouldn't have to go through all this agony and worry. Don't you know it hurts me to see you trying to make light of a very serious problem?"

She pulled herself free and reached for her now cold coffee, sipping at it to gain time. "Do you really want me to marry you in order to solve my housing problem?"

"I want you to marry me for any reason at all."

Now it was her turn to grow serious. "How can I marry you when I'm so deep in debt that I may never get out? I thought it was bad before, owing the Filmores, but now I'm going to have to mortgage the nursery to replace the house."

"Why does the house have to be replaced? You and the girls aren't going to need it, love. You'll be here."

She looked at him, eyes worried. Would they? Was that what she wanted?

"Even if the girls and I don't end up back there, or maybe I should say, especially if we don't, the nursery is going to have to have a live-in manager. It's too much for Abe to handle on his own. Ideally, Evelyn and her family should live there. Just as, ideally, Abe should have inherited the business, and been able to pass it on to them in time."

But even as she made those lame excuses, she knew that she wanted the house rebuilt for her own sake; no matter what, she wanted something that belonged to her and the girls, a bolt hole, she supposed, a place to run to if they ever had to run.

She smiled wryly and pushed that thought away.

"Maybe a miracle will happen and I'll be awarded a contract to do a new golf course or something."

He raised his brows. "Have you bid on one?"

"Of course not. We're talking miracles here."

He ruffled her short, curly hair and grinned at her. "Just looking at the transformation from featureless amoeba to vibrant, incredibly beautiful elf makes me believe in miracles too."

And an hour later, if miracles had then seemed in short supply to Sandy, in spite of her brave words, they no longer did.

The generosity of those who had seen the film of the fire on the six o'clock news, and had responded so quickly and overwhelmingly, was not to be believed, only she had to believe it because it was happening. She stood at the garage door, staring in at the sacks and boxes and stacks of items that had begun arriving in the early evening and were still coming in and piling up.

There were stuffed animals, other toys, books, games, clothing, linens, dishes and pots and pans. There was a nearly-new sofa and matching chair, an upside-down rocking chair hung atop a television set beside a pair of bunk beds. There were pillows and scatter mats and knick-knacks and home preserves. There was even a brown burlap sack of potatoes and—heaven help her—a sewing machine! The driveway was lined with cars and trucks still disgorging people and things.

Sandy shook hands, murmured words of thanks, stared bemused at the box that was filling with dollar bills, fives, tens, twenties, and loose change. Her throat ached with tears she tried not to shed, but she was unable to hold them back when an old man pressed a twenty into her hand and set a gilt-framed oval mirror on the ground outside the stuffed garage. "Your granny was a good member of this community, missy, and I'm glad to be able to help out when one of hers needs it."

"Now, you get along up to bed," said Mrs. Long kindly when the tears, and the procession of donations, had stopped. "You've had a long, tough day. I'll bring you hot milk."

The hot milk, laced with brandy, was good, and Sandy drank it all. Mrs. Long was right. It did relax her and help her sleep, but she didn't stay asleep for long. Waking with a start, she listened for the crackle of flames. Getting out of bed, she checked around for smoke. Opening Roger's door, she checked to be sure he was all right.

He slept so soundly, his cheek flushed and moist in the dim glow of the night-light near the floor. His hair was sweat-dampened and curling, and Sandy smoothed it off his brow. He smiled around his thumb, turning in to her caress, and she backed away, not wanting to awaken him but needing to stay near, to be in contact with another human being.

Rick found her there and drew her silently into the hall. In the faint light coming through the window over the stairs, he held her hands away from her body, looking at her slim form in the satin nightie he had bought for her. He wanted to press it to her skin, mold it to her body, feel her shape through it. Desire rose up in him, making him catch his breath, and as if she could read his mind, she took his hands and placed them over her breasts.

Taking her hand, he walked down the stairs, across the living room, and into his bedroom. His short robe was silk, she knew, feeling it slither down as she untied it and pushed it off his shoulders. His chest hair rubbed against the satin of her gown, tantalizing her nipples through the fabric, and she slipped one strap off her shoulder, then the other, and shimmied out of it.

"Love me," she whispered.

And he did, but long before dawn she had slipped away and gone back to her own room, leaving him lying on his back, hands behind his head, feeling bereft and wondering how long it would have to be this way, she sleeping in her bed, he in his, one or the other of them sneaking out at night to visit. Not long, he told himself. He wouldn't take it for long.

If the donations of the first night had been amazing, what happened over the next several days was downright mind-boggling. A crew turned up and began to tear down the blackened remains of the house. As truck loads of junk headed out, truck loads of new building material headed in.

Sandy tried to stop it, but was brushed aside with assurances that it was all donated material, all donated time.

It was just as well, she thought, because the bank was still waffling on her loan, saying that even with the nursery for collateral, they needed more time to consider. The profit picture wasn't all they might ask for.

And when the girls returned home, their picture on the front page of the morning paper brought a new rash of donations, from more toys and books that had clearly been much-loved members of families, and used clothing, to quite a few new outfits from local stores. And as a result of the publicity, landscaping jobs came in. If it was a case of "Oh, give the poor woman the job, she needs it," Sandy didn't care. Her work, she knew, would stand up under any scrutiny; all she'd ever asked for was a chance to prove her abilities. This was her chance. She took it.

"I just have to move back down the hill," she said one Sunday afternoon, sorting through the garage, trying to introduce some order into the chaos.

"Leave that alone," said Rick, tugging her out into the sunlight. "You can't move back down the hill. The house isn't ready. Hell, there are no partitions. At least let the plasterers have their day before you put yourself and all this clutter in their way. Besides, your insistence on moving back there before we get married is just plain crazy. There's no need for it. And when are we going to tell the kids?"

"You promised," she said. "You said you wouldn't push me, Rick, and you've done it all along."

"But you are going to marry me, aren't you?"

"I . . . I don't know. I suppose so. Maybe. Someday. But . . ."

"The girls have been home nearly two weeks," he said. "And you promised we'd tell all three of them when they were back."

"That was before. Rick, give me more time."

"I'm not letting you back out, Sandy. We are going to get married. Sooner or later, we are."

She sighed gustily as they went into the foyer.

"I'll be a financial drag on you."

"Let me worry about that," he said, taking her head between his hands and kissing her loudly.

"Don't," she whispered, jerking away as Jenny came in, closely followed by Pam, who had Roger in tow. Pam always had Roger in tow.

"Hi, Mom. Hi, Rick. When are we going swimming?"

"In two minutes. As soon as your mother changes."

"Into what?" she asked. "I haven't even thought about buying a new swimsuit, and if there's one out in the garage, it would take until Christmas to find it."

"Go look on your bed." Rick and Jennifer exchanged glances and grinned.

"All right, what are you guys up to? I warn you, if it's something indecent, I won't wear it."

"You'll love it, Mom," said Jenny. "Won't she, Pammy?"

Pam bit her lower lip and looked down at her bare feet before glancing up, worriedly, at her mother. "It's your colors."

"Now, why doesn't that reassure me?" mumbled Sandy, but she ran up the stairs.

"Oh . . . my . . . goodness!" she said aloud, staring down at the bikini. It was the tiniest thing she had ever seen. It was black with turquoise diagonal stripes and was constructed of nothing more than strings and scraps.

She put it on and stepped to the mirror.

It was indecent. It was shocking. It was so immodest she nearly blushed there in her room all by herself.

It also looked terrific. She grinned and struck a hip-cocked pose, hand on waist, head flung back, and then giggled at herself. Picking up the short cover-up that was still lying on the bed, she buttoned it and went downstairs to where Rick had all three kids securely buckled into the backseat of the Buick.

"It fit okay?" he asked casually as he swung onto the road.

"Oh, sure, just fine," she said, equally casual, while a flutter of excitement curled in her stomach. Oh, how she wanted to see his reaction to her in this bikini. Her first bikini. And very likely, her last. Because when Rick saw her in it, he'd probably have several fits and take her home right away to put on a gunny sack.

But his lazy, half-shuttered eyes glittered with what might have been approval for a moment when she peeled off her cover by the pool. "It does fit well" was his only comment before he dove in to cavort with the children.

Pleased not to have to fight against being packed off home as if she were too disgusting to be seen in public, and disgruntled that Rick had paid so little attention to her in the bikini, Sandy spread their blanket near a big tree that would provide shade later, and lay on her front soaking up the rays. Presently, a few drops of cold water on her back made her lift her head and roll over. Rick sat behind her and lifted her up to lean on his folded thigh. She closed her eyes as his fingers beat a little path from her knee to her hip.

"I think we're going to have to have a little talk about that vault again."

She laughed, well-pleased. "Oh, so you do like it. From the reaction I got, I thought you saw it as just another bikini among the hundreds already here."

"Lady, I reacted. If I'd stayed out of the water for one more second, you and everyone else here would have known exactly what kind of reaction you, in that bikini, evoked in me."

"I'm glad."

"I'm glad you like it too. Glad you wore it. There's

a navy blue maillot in your top drawer just in case you refused this one completely."

"You rat," she said mildly, closing her eyes, enjoying the feel of the sun on her face, the warmth of his leg against her back, the gentle movement of his hands in her hair.

"I thought you might be afraid I'd attract the wrong kind of attention," she said quietly a few minutes later.

He understood at once. "I trust you. And I am very, very proud of you and the way you look. When are you going to realize that I am not Alex? When are you going to stop expecting his reactions from me?"

She didn't reply, and he let the subject go, continuing to run his fingers through her short hair.

Something fell on her shoulder. He brushed it off. She opened her eyes. "What are you doing?"

"Romancing my lady."

"Hey! You can't do that!" She saw what he had done.

"Can't romance my lady?"

"Can't pick flowers in the park."

"Daisies aren't flowers," he scoffed. "They grow wild. They're fair game. Now, sit still. You're knocking your garland off. Ah, there." He crawled around on his hands and knees to look at her.

"Gorgeous. You look like a woodland nymph leaning over a sylvan pool."

Sandy laughed. "If I leaned over any kind of pool, poetically sylvan or not, my garland would fall off, which would be just as well because for sure some kind of official is going to come and run you in for picking flowers in the park."

"I didn't pick any flowers," he said innocently. "These must have fallen from the tree to land there, enhancing my lady's hair. Now, what kind of official could argue with that?"

"The kind who knows that daisies don't grow on chestnut trees and hence cannot fall off . . . oh! Stop that!"

"I love the taste of suntan lotion," he said, tipping her backward until she lay on the blanket with him propped beside her, nuzzling her neck. The garland tilted over one eye. She left it there as a sunshade.

"Rick, don't."

"Why not? The kids aren't looking, and what if they were? Jen asked me yesterday when we were going to get married. Did you think we were fooling them? That they haven't figured out we're in love?"

Sandy raised her little, fuzzy eyebrows, blinked her stubbly little lashes, and shoved the garland up off her brow, ignoring the questions. "I'll have to have a talk with that child,"she said.

"Don't bother." He smiled, running a fingertip up and down—but mostly down—her flat abdomen. "I explained."

Sandy shivered under his touch. "What, exactly, did you explain?"

"I told her I'm working on it. How'm I doin'?"

He moved his finger around her side, slipping it under the elastic of her bikini bottoms.

"Cut it out," she said, squirming, trying to capture his hand and hold it still. He was elusive and quick. She shut her eyes against the sun. And against the exquisite torture of his touch.

"Tell me you'll marry me and I will," he teased.

"Yeah, Mom, tell him. This is getting embarrassing," said Jennifer, dripping all over them. Sandy sprang back.

"Now look what you've done!" she said furiously to Rick, rolling completely out of his reach. "You've embarrassed the kids."

"I'm not embarrassed, Mom," Pamela said, being careful not to drip on the blanket as she got Roger's towel and handed it to him before reaching for her own.

"I think it's kinda cute."

Nine

"Cute?" Somehow that made Sandy even madder, and she snapped at all of them, "There's nothing cute about it, and Rick's old enough to know better!"

"Aren't *you*, Sammy?" Roger asked innocently, making his father snort with laughter. "How old are you?"

"She's gonna be thirty tomorrow!" chorused Sandy's big-mouthed children, and she glared at them.

"Is that a fact?" Rick grinned. "Well, now. And she never said a word. Trying to keep it a secret, Sandy?" He turned back to the kids. "So what are we going to do to celebrate the occasion?"

"We are going to do nothing," said Sandy crossly. "And tomorrow is Monday. I have to work."

"You aren't going to have to work all day. You're getting bad-tempered, Ms. Aabab. Too much sun and too little food." Rick grabbed a corner of the blanket and dragged her, blanket, and picnic basket into the shade. "Who's hungry?"

Everyone was, and the food disappeared as the four conspirators whispered together. Sandy sat apart, leaning against the rough bark of the tree.

"People don't celebrate thirtieth birthdays," she said huffily after several minutes of listening to the whispers and giggles. "At least this person doesn't. I have a crew ready to work on the Gregerson place, and the Gregersons are in a hurry, so we'll be at it from sunup to sundown."

"Gregerson?" Rick asked with a frown. "It's not in this neighborhood, is it? I haven't seen a new sign of yours up locally for a while."

Sandy shook her head. "It's about seven miles up the gorge from Troutdale. A summer home." Then, feeling guilty at the reproachful glances from all three kids, she added, "I'm sorry, gang, but I do have to work, and if my birthday falls on a workday, there's nothing I can do about it."

"If you married my daddy," said Roger, "then you could stay home all day and eat cookies with me and Mrs. Long and have parties anytime you want."

Sandy ruffled his hair. "You, too, huh? No way, pal. If I were married, I'd still want my job. I like to work."

Roger looked mournful. "Don't you like my daddy?"

She leapt to her feet. "I like your daddy just fine, but that has nothing to do with me and my job!" With that, she tore toward the pool, ignoring the three childish voices behind her shouting, "You just *ate*!"

"No," said Sandy impatiently, leaping to the side of the boy who was part of the crew she had hand-clearing the Gregerson property. "I told you to leave things like that, Freddy. Don't you recognize wild columbine when you see it?" He should. She'd showed him four times already. Freddy, she was begining to realize, was not bright. This was the same kid who had not ten minutes ago destroyed several fine specimens of Oregon grape.

"I thought you were all botany students," she said, her mouth grim, sweat running down her face. "Can't you identify anything on your own?"

"I'm only first year," he said, "and, well, things look different from what they do in a book."

"Freddy, we are hand-clearing so as not to disturb the valuable wild-flower specimens that grow here. So, please, if you're in doubt, ask. Okay?" She tried for a smile, felt it slipping away, and strode past the dumb kid before she was tempted to brain him with a shovel.

Immediately, she felt like a rat. It wasn't poor Freddy's fault she was in a foul mood and had been all day. But he was trying. Unfortunately, though, he had big, clumsy feet and trampled on things before he even knew they were there. She wondered if she should try to teach him, or if she should fire him.

Ordinarily, she wouldn't even have asked herself that kind of question. She'd merely have kept him working beside her and made sure he didn't do any damage, at least while there was some hope that he might learn something from the work. But today, feeling as sore and as let down as she did, as angry and hurt inside, she didn't have the patience Freddy required.

Half an hour later she sent the crew to the nearest town for their dinner, asking only that they bring her a cold drink. She was feeling too miserable to think about food.

Her kids had forgotten her. Rick, all right, that she could understand. She had said that she didn't want her birthday celebrated, but . . . By tradition, birthday gifts were left on the kitchen table at night for the recipient to find in the morning, only this morning there had been nothing for her.

Oh, knock it off, she told herself. *You're acting like three, not thirty.*

Thirty! God, she'd never dreamed she'd ever be thirty. People were so right. Thirty was a traumatic age. All day she'd been aware of it, and age was something she'd never concerned herself with unduly. Ten years ago she'd been twenty and young and just beginning to experience life—not that the experiences had been all that good—but they hadn't been all that bad either. She had two wonderful little daughters. Yet, those ten years had flown by; in ten more she'd be forty.

God, I'm almost forty! How did people survive being that old? Her kids would be nearly nineteen, probably they'd have left home and she'd be alone. No, no. She'd have Rick and Roger. Wouldn't she? Oh, Lord, she didn't know. What if it didn't work out? There she'd be, a middle-aged divorcee who spent her days designing gardens for other people's children to grow up in. She'd work all day, come home at night to a silent, empty house, make small and solitary meals, read a book and go to bed early only to wake up the next morning and start the same sequence all over again. Oh, once a month or so, one of the girls might call and chat for a minute, but then need to run off and do something more important than talking to her mother. A date, maybe, an important exam. Then, later, exciting, sophisticated lives. If it were Jenny, she'd likely have two minutes between journalism assignments, call from the airport, where she'd just arrived back from covering a war in one spot before she flew on to another.

Pam. When would she have time to call? She'd be so busy with all her lovely babies that Sandy had only seen once because Pammy was married to the ambassador to—

Wiping tears from her face with a grubby hand, Sandy attacked a thick tangle of blackberry vines with her mattock. Left alone, they'd overwhelm the Gregersons' neat little A-frame as Sleeping Beauty's castle had been overwhelmed.

If she lived in a castle and was trapped by a wall of thorns, would a handsome prince come tearing his way in to get her, she wondered idly, then grimaced in disgust. *What the hell would I want with a handsome prince? The minute I kissed him, he'd turn into a frog.*

Only, she knew that wasn't fair. Rick hadn't. Or if he had, it had been a temporary aberration. Since the day after the fire, when he'd acted like such an arrogant jerk, he'd changed and become the epitome of liberated manhood, willing to have her do what she had to do, taking what time she could spare. And mostly without complaint. Surely it would be safe to marry him. he wouldn't revert to caveman, not now that he knew how she hated it, how she valued her independence. She wanted him and needed him and she really should agree to marry him—soon.

She would have agreed to anything ten minutes later when she saw his car come barreling up the hill, stop, and spill out three laughing kids. They came running to her, and she took off her gloves to scoop all three of them into her arms, her gaze flying up to Rick's face.

"Did you really think we'd take you at your word?"

She nodded, and managed a wobbly smile as the kids ran back to the car. "I thought the girls had forgotten." She shrugged to show how little it really mattered. "It's kind of a silly tradition we've developed over the years. We leave each other birthday gifts on the kitchen table."

LIGHT ANOTHER CANDLE • 155

"I know—now, and it's my fault they didn't. I wanted this to be the same as my family tradition. When do you open Christmas presents?"

"Before breakfast," she said, lifting her chin as if daring him to argue.

"Good. No conflict there."

Dammit, how could he be so confident that it was all going to happen the way he said it would? She wanted to ask, but the kids were back, bearing brightly if inexpertly wrapped gifts, and Sandy opened them, exclaiming over them happily. When she was finished, Pam turned her big eyes up to Rick and said. "What did you get for Mom?"

"Pam!" chided Sandy. Something like that she might have expected from Jenny, but not from Pamela.

But Rick only smiled and said, "She gets that later, at home. Now let's bring on dinner. This is one starved-looking lady we have here."

He had even brought a jug of water for her to wash in, along with soap, towel, and basin. But was she even permitted to do that herself? Oh, no. Rick did it, over her spluttering protests. He washed her face and hands while the kids staggered around, spreading the picnic over the Gregersons' front porch.

When Sandy was clean and refreshed, Rick ceremoniously placed another garland on her head, this one made of pink rosebuds and ivy, and she wished for a mirror suddenly. He arranged the children around and behind her and took photographs from different angles before turning the camera over to Jenny and getting down beside Sandy, his arm around her, his cheek close to hers.

"For the family album," he said, tucking the camera down into the side of the picnic basket and then pouring her a glass of white wine. "Pammy, is your mother's plate ready?"

It was, and she was served on the finest china, with silver cutlery, while the rest of them made do with paper and plastic. On the tray circling her plate was yet another wreath of flowers. All this special attention made her feel foolish, she told herself, wondering why "foolish" was so close to "pampered" and "beloved" in her mind.

When the main course was finished, Pam and Jenny carried the cake over, and Roger, with his father's help, handed Sandy a beribboned knife to cut it with.

"What a beautiful cake!" Sandy said.

"We made it," Jenny said, bouncing with pride. "Rick did most of it, but we helped. Isn't it pretty, Mom? I've never seen a cake with green icing before."

"That's because you've hardly ever seen a cake before, unless your granny baked it," Sandy replied wryly. "Thank you all. It's the most wonderful cake I've ever had. And the best birthday."

"We wanted to put candles on, Mom," said Pam, "but Rick said no."

Sandy turned toward Rick and saw the sadness

in his expression. He wasn't giving her any more candles until she gave him the one he wanted—the big one, the bright one, the one that would shine even in the strongest sun. And so far all she'd offered him was one that shone just in the night.

"Rick was right," she said, hardly over a whisper. "The . . . wind might have blown them out."

"I'll expect thirty-six on mine," said Rick over the heads of the children. "On the twelfth of October."

Then, when it was all gathered up and stowed away, Rick called the kids. "Come on, you guys. Say good night to your mother. She has lots more work to do and we've held her up long enough."

"Okay, Daddy," said Roger obediently.

"Okay, Daddy," said the girls together, Jenny with an impudent grin, Pam without a change of expression, as if she called Rick Daddy every day.

Sandy's gasp cut into the sudden silence and then she said sharply, "Jennifer! Pamela! Rick is *not* your daddy and you will not call him that! Do I make myself clear?"

"But, Mom!" Jennifer burst into tears along with her sister. In sympathy Roger cried, too, and clung to his father's leg, eyes wide and startled on Sandy's furious face. "We were only kidding!"

"Well, I'm not kidding, Jennifer! And don't you ever forget it!"

With a last, disbelieving look at Sandy, Rick scooped his son up and ushered the girls back to the car. He got behind the wheel and pulled out, not bothering to look at her again. She stood there, the circlet of roses and ivy on her head growing heavier and heavier until she flung it off and picked up her mattock again, chopping wildly and blindly into the blackberry vines.

Her rage still had not abated by the time she got home. Carefully, she had hung on to it, finding in it some relief from the guilt she felt. The kids were not accustomed to being shrieked at like that, but it was all Rick's fault. If he hadn't made it appear—deliberately, she was certain—that he was addressing all three of them when he said "your mother," then the girls wouldn't have picked up on his game. He must have been encouraging them, using them to get at her, and he had promised not to push. If that wasn't pushing, she didn't know what was!

"Who the hell gave my children permission to call you Daddy?" she demanded by way of greeting when she found him sitting on the deck as if waiting for her.

He stood up. "Not me," he said evenly. "And as Jenny told you, they were only kidding."

"That's not the kind of joke I find amusing," she ranted, "and I want it stopped!"

"What you want is a shower, a drink, and a good long rest," he said, refusing to be provoked.

"Dammit, don't you tell me what I want, Richard Gearing! I am thirty years old and I know what I want without your telling me!"

"All right, then, what do you want?"

She stared at him, mouth agape, as she tried to think of something to say. She closed it. Then, opening it again, she said, "I want . . . I want . . . a shower, a drink, and a good long hug."

With a laugh he caught her close and gave her the hug first.

"I'm so sorry, Rick. That wonderful birthday you gave me, and I went and blew it and hurt the kids, scared them, made them cry."

"It's okay, love. They understand that that's a bit of a sore point with you. I explained. And now that they understand, they won't kid around like that anymore. And I'm sorry, too, that you were upset on your birthday. According to family tradition, that's not supposed to happen." He kissed her until she shoved him away, knowing what came next. Wanting it.

"Rick . . . I smell!"

"Mmm, like the outdoors, and earth and grass. But go have a shower if it'll make you feel better. I'll fix you a drink."

After she'd showered and changed into a loose caftan, Sandy looked in on the kids. She bent and kissed her daughters, silently apologizing to them. They both smiled in their sleep, so she felt much better. Roger lay on his side looking like a small, dark cherub. She stroked his hair, kissed him, and left.

"Here's your drink," Rick said, reaching out a hand to pull her down onto the swing with him.

As she sat, he lifted her feet onto his lap and began massaging them.

"Why are you driving yourself like this?" he asked. "What happened to 'design and supervision'? Isn't that what you said you were going to concentrate on?"

"Yes, but . . ." He simply didn't understand how she hated being in debt.

"But what?" he asked, his hands riding higher and higher on her legs, fingers pressing and swirling, fluttering over sensitive nerve endings, soothing sore muscles.

"But the harder I work, the sooner I'll be out of debt."

"Honey, I think you put too much importance on your debts. Sure, I know you want to pay them off, and I know you'll do it. But are the Filmores sending you weekly dunning letters?"

"No. Of course not. But they've been patient so long. Rick, they aren't wealthy people. They had to borrow in order to bury their son and look after me and the girls. I know they scrimped and cut corners to pay back the credit union, so the faster I can pay them back, the better I'll feel. I hate feeling like a parasite, being a financial albatross. I truly want to come to you free and clear and able to hold up my end of things, and while I'm sending every spare dime to the Filmores, I don't think I'll ever be truly free of the past."

He was thoughtful and silent while he continued to massage her legs and feet. Finally, he said,

"I want you to be free of your past. Not because it bothers me, but because I know how it worries you. All right, then, I won't argue about the hours you put in, or the number of jobs you take. But I do want you to know this: There is no need now, and unless something very, very strange and unforeseen happens, there will never be any need for you to 'hold up your end of things.' I can and will support you and all three of our children. It's what I want to do. It's what I see as my privilege, not my obligation. It makes me feel good about myself to know that I can care for those I love. I want to fight off the tigers trying to get into the cave. I want to drag home the mastodon carcass. I want to—"

"Club me over the head and drag me home by the hair?" she interrupted with a laugh. "Rick, believe me, I'm not out there working because I think you're incapable of looking after us, but only because the debt is mine. The benefits are mine. And I have to take care of it on my own."

"Okay," he said softly, his hands moving back down her legs to her feet. "Now do you want your next birthday present?"

She wriggled her toes in pleasure. "You mean there's more? I thought this was it. It's enough, you know."

"No, it's not," he said, placing her feet on the cushions of the glider and bending to pull a small wrapped box from underneath.

Carefully, she untied the ribbons, opened the

paper, and lifted the lid. Inside was nothing more than a note. She smiled as she followed the directions it contained, going to look on top of the refrigerator, then on the third chair from the left in the dining room, in the blue vase on the table in the hall. From there she was led upstairs, back down to the utility room, into the living room and then outside. More notes hung on trees, were tucked under paving stones, held by small rocks to the steps leading to the gazebo on the bluff and, finally, as she had long ago begun to expect she would, she found a huge, beribboned package sitting on the floor of the gazebo. The flickering of candles in hurricane lamps danced in Rick's golden hair and blue eyes. He looked as excited as any of the three children had earlier in the day when she opened their gifts.

Sitting down on one of the thickly cushioned seats built in to seven sides of the octagonal structure, she tore open the paper and saw the loose sides of the box fall outward to reveal a twisted, beautifully shaped bonsai oak tree that had to be at least thirty years old, the age her other one would have been.

"Oh, Rick," she cried. "How lovely! Thank you. Thank you for doing this for me."

She lifted out the little oak tree and held it to the light. "I felt so terrible about losing the other one. In many ways, it was the greatest loss because I knew how long my grandmother had cared for it on my behalf."

Getting to her feet, she stood the tree on the table and slipped into his arms, lifting her face to kiss him. "I love you."

He pulled back an inch, his eyes no longer looking excited, but oddly apprehensive now. "There's more."

She smiled. "I don't need more."

Setting her back from him, he turned the small potted tree in the light and for the first time she saw the shiny ornaments hanging from it suspended on fine threads.

Pearl earrings, to match the pearl necklace she had left, with a wedding gown, in the house to burn. Diamond earrings, small and dainty but incredibly expensive-looking. Jade earrings, smooth and cool to the touch, and one pair of opals, dangling to capture rainbows out of thin air and cast them into her starry eyes as Rick turned the twisted tree for her to look.

And then, while her heart went still in her chest, he lifted an oak leaf.

"Rick . . ." Her whisper was a small, choked sound.

"Please," he said, his voice husky and ragged. "Oh, Sandy, don't tell me no." He unhooked the diamond solitaire and held it out toward her on his palm, his face pale, his eyes still filled with apprehension.

Lifting her left hand, watching it tremble, she parted her fingers. The ring, as he slipped it onto her finger, felt cold, but it took on her body heat quickly as she warmed to his exuberant embrace. Laughing, he swung her around and around inside the little gazebo, flipping seat cushions onto the floor, making a bed for them.

"And now, my dearest darling, how would you like to spend the rest of your birthday?"

"What?" She grinned up at him quickly, willing to glance away from the beautiful ring for only a moment. "You mean you don't have a handy tradition to cover that?"

"No, but if you give me a minute or two, I'm sure I'll be able to dream one up."

To Sandy's intense delight, he was.

Life, she decided as he tucked her into her own bed hours later before going back downstairs to his, was more wonderful than she had any right to expect. And soon, very, very soon, that big bed in the master bedroom would belong to both of them. And once that had happened, she promised herself as she snuggled down under her covers, nothing was going to change it. Ever.

Ten

Had she been tempting fate in making such a rash promise to herself, Sandy wondered a few days later after experiencing devastating pain. When it had faded to numbness and she could finally think, she decided the gods must have wanted to see her writhe.

And, oh, was she writhing!

It had all started so innocently, too, the day she had agreed with Rick that she shouldn't go out to any of her job sites, but stay home and take it easy. Taking it easy to Sandy meant getting her own place cleaned up, clearing away some of the construction debris now that the exterior was finished and only the interior was left to do.

Chunks of left-over building material lay helter-skelter on the singed earth. Pieces of metal strapping that had held bundles of lumber together glinted in the sun. There were odd bits of unrecognizable burned things that had been trampled into the ground and were now forcing their way out, foul reminders of the horror that had been.

She began tearing at the mess, flinging it into the back of the pickup, tossing in bits of two-by-fours, broken boards, fragments of dishes. The strapping kept catching on nails and rough edges, and she tugged at it, careful that it not cut through her gloves, pulling out yards of it, fighting its kinked, snaking recalcitrance. One piece snapped free, almost slapping her in the face, and a piece of paper attached to it flipped at her before hanging still as if saying "Read me!" right before her eyes.

She read it. Across the top was written in very distinctive lettering *R.J. Gearing*. A huge sum of money appeared below. The paper was torn, rain-blurred, boot-marked, but still legible, and it didn't need to be complete for her to understand the half-obliterated rubber stamp mark that said *Paid in Full*.

The world receded as she stood there, slowly crumpling the paper in her hand. For a long time she saw nothing but the words she had read, and the figures, and she shook her head to clear it, wondering what she could do to ease this terrible pain inside, and then, in time, knowing what she had to do.

• • •

Rick pounded his fist on the table, making the scrap of shipping label bounce, the check flutter, the diamond ring dance, creating a musical sound on the wood.

"Dammit, are you saying that because of this you're going back on your promise to marry me? That's the stupidest, weakest excuse I have ever heard, Sandra Aabab, and I'm not buying it! If you can't see that I bought that lumber out of love and compassion and caring, then I guess you're right and we don't belong together! What the hell's the difference between my doing what I did and the building trades people donating their time and labor? How does my donation come across as unwelcome charity and the things given you by other members of the community turn out to be gifts of kindness? Does the fact that I did it out of love cheapen it somehow? Make what I paid dirty money? What's the difference, Sandy? Tell me."

"The difference is that I wasn't sleeping with the building trades union. That I don't feel like a . . . a . . ."

"Whore? Is that the word you can't seem to say? Did I ever call you that? Did I ever make you feel like that?"

"No, but believe me, I have been called that!" she cried raggedly. "For years I was called that and worse, and I swore I'd never be put into that position again. You had no right, Rick. How can I marry a man who lies to me? A man who went behind my back to do something I'd hate because he knew if he asked me or offered openly, I'd have refused? You knew how I'd hate it if I ever found out. And you knew I wouldn't have accepted your ring and your proposal of marriage if I'd had this kind of debt. Well, now I owe the bank, but somehow, that's better than owing you. I pay my own way. I told you that! Nobody does it for me. I look after my own obligations, and if you can't live with that, then stay the hell out of my life."

He followed her to the door. "Oh, yes, believe me, I'm out of your life. I've been stung too often by the poison you carry around inside. I just hope that you grow up and get over it someday, because otherwise you're going to die a lonely old lady."

He shut the door and she strode away, head held high, back down the path to the gate, and the unfinished, uncomfortable house filled with boxes full of stuff with no place to be stored, and two children who resented her having snatched them so abruptly out of the comfort of Rick's house.

Behind her, she heard Rick open the door again and call after her, "And take your raven with you. He seems to have forgotten where he lives."

But Never lived where Never chose, and he had decided that he was Mrs. Long's bird. Not that Sandy didn't see him; he sailed back and forth up and down the gully of the creek as regularly as the kids let the gate clang shut behind them. Rick and Sandy's estrangement didn't keep Roger from Sandy or Pam and Jenny from Rick, a fact of life that made her growing loneliness harder and harder to bear.

One week passed, then two. Sleep was something that came only irregularly and for short periods. Sandy dragged herself out of bed, got the girls off to school, and went to work. Not that there was a lot. People were beginning to batten down for fall now that September was here.

The girls' birthday party came and went. Roger arrived with a gift. "How come that little kid came?" asked one of Jenny's friends.

"We want him here," said Pam. "He's sort of like our brother."

Sandy went into the kitchen so the children wouldn't see her breaking down.

"I can't go on," she told herself. "I can't live like this for even one more day." But she did. She went on for three more days and then, one night when both the girls were sleeping over at a friend's, she knew she had to see Rick.

"See me? What for?" He didn't sound angry. He just sounded indifferent. "What do you want to see me for, Sandy?" he repeated when she failed to answer his question.

"I . . . miss you." She gripped the phone tightly, making her hand ache. It didn't matter. She was one big ache all the time anyway. "I want to tell you I'm sorry about the way I acted. Of course your having paid for the lumber was no different from what anyone else did."

"Wasn't it?"

"No. I mean, yes. Yes, it was different. It was better. You did it because you loved me."

"Yes, I did."

Yes, he did it for that reason, or yes, he did love her—had loved her—past tense?

"Rick, would you come down here, please? Or could I come up there?"

"Mrs. Long's out this evening, and I can't leave Roger. You can't leave the girls, so I guess that's that." He didn't seem to care one bit.

If only she could see his face, touch him. Talking on the phone wasn't good enough. "The girls are both sleeping over at a friend's tonight. So . . . is it okay if I come up?"

He didn't answer right away. Her chest ached. Her eyes burned. Her throat was one long column of pain. "Rick?" she whispered through it.

She knew he was there because she heard him sigh. "No, I don't see much point in it, Sandy."

"I—I want to marry you," she blurted out.

Again, there was a long silence before he said, "Do you? For how long this time? I mean, before you changed your mind? Before I did something that you hated and you backed out on me again? How many times do you think I can take that?"

"Oh, God, Rick! Just give me a chance! That's all I need. I won't let you down again!"

"I want more than anything to believe that, my

darling," he said, and she suspected he was fighting tears. She'd stopped fighting, recognizing a losing battle when she faced one. "But how can I? How can I know that you won't find some other excuse to back down on me? You don't have enough faith in me, Sandy. You've never had any real trust. Love is trust. I want a wife who can share with me and who will let me share with her. This isn't about lumber and debts, it's about nothing more than belief in each other. I don't want you as long as you're afraid to let me give you things in case I act as if I've bought you with them. I don't want you unless I can be sure you trust me all the way—unless I'm sure I can trust you just as much."

"Rick . . . Rick . . ." she said, her voice thick with tears. "How can I tell you? How can I show you? What do I have to do?"

"I don't know, Sandy. I really don't know." And she believed him. She believed that if he could think of a way for them to get back together, he'd tell her, ask anything of her that would make it good between them again. At least she believed that, believed in his love enough to be sure he'd do whatever was needed. So it was true. He didn't know where the path back together lay anymore than she did.

"I guess it's a problem I'm going to have to solve on my own," she said.

"I guess so," he said softly. "Good night, love."

Sandy sat long into the night wondering how in

the world she was ever going to devise a way to float a candle upstream.

"Mom, aren't you going to eat your cereal?" asked Pam, taking a spoonful of her own. "It's getting mushy."

Sandy took a spoonful. It was mushy. It was all she could do to swallow.

"Leave her alone, Pammy," said Jennifer. "She's pining."

"I am not! And where did you get a word like that?"

"Mr. Freemantle's reading us a book about a dog that got lost and won't eat even though his new owner gives him steak and other stuff. He's pining for his old owner just like you are."

"I am not a dog," Sandy said, shoving her bowl aside, "and Rick was never my owner. Now, eat and brush your teeth or you'll miss the bus."

Jenny put her bowl into the sink. "Mom, we're going to the opera next Saturday. Can we have new shoes?"

Sandy stared at her eldest—by eleven minutes—daughter. "The opera?"

"The symphony, Jen," said Pam. "And we want to wear those long yellow dresses Nesbitt's Fine Fashions sent us, Mom. So we need new shoes. Elspeth says ladies dress for the symphony."

"Do tell! And who is Elspeth?"

"You know her. Miss Franklin, from the college.

She and Rick are friends. She gave him the tickets."

Miss Franklin? Elspeth Franklin? With the long, blond hair and the incredible green eyes and the body that just wouldn't quit? That Elspeth Franklin? The Elspeth Franklin who played seven musical instruments and spoke nine languages and had an I.Q. somewhere around the altitude of Mount Hood if all accounts of her brilliance were true? Elspeth Franklin, who probably didn't even have to use deodorant because her body was too perfect to sweat? That Elspeth Franklin? And she was giving Rick tickets to symphonies?

"Mom? Can we have new shoes?"

"Oh, yes. Sure. It was . . . nice of Miss Franklin to give Rick the tickets for you. You must write her polite thank-you notes."

"Oh, we thanked her already. Yesterday. At the pool." Jenny shook her head in mazement. "Boy, can Elspeth ever swim! She almost beat Rick in a race."

But had the good sense to lose, Sandy thought, and said aloud, "Jen, I prefer you to call her Miss Franklin. It's rude for you to use her first name. After all, you're young girls and she's an older woman." *But not "older" enough! She might have two or three years on Rick, but that surely wouldn't matter to either of them.*

"She said we could, Mom. I mean, Roger does, and he's even younger, but she's a friend of his father's so Roger gets to call her by her first name."

Sandy didn't argue. It was too hard to talk with her mouth full of cotton balls.

After the girls had gone, she sat, chin in her hands, staring at the bits of cereal, the little slops of milk, the toast crumbs and butter smears on the table. Finally, she became aware that tears were running down her face and wetting her fingers. The salt of them stung in small cuts in her skin. She looked at her hands, seeing them as small and square and utilitarian, totally unlike the long, slender white fingers that Elspeth Franklin sported, with bright red nails that were never chipped or broken.

How could a short female landscaper who knew next to nothing about anything except plants and soil composition and drainage possibly compete with a tall, beautiful musician who was also a linguist, who had an intellect as well as a gorgeous body, and knew what the kids should wear to the symphony? She couldn't, and she knew it. Hell, if it had been left to her, her kids would be going dressed in school clothes because she didn't know any better, never having been within six miles of a symphony, and they'd have been embarrassed half to death.

She got to her feet and wiped the table mindlessly, wondering how long Rick had been seeing Elspeth. Was Elspeth nice to Roger? Did she hold him and rock him when he missed his mother? She didn't want to think of what Elspeth might be doing for Rick.

Suddenly, she flung the dishcloth across the kitchen. It hit the refrigerator with a splat and slid to the floor. She left it lying where it fell as she wiped her face on the sleeves of her workshirt. "No, dammit, she can't horn in! She can't have Rick! And she can't be Roger's stepmother because I am not going to let her!"

Standing in the middle of her messy kitchen, Sandy felt determination sweep over her, filling her with resolve, but suddenly her up became a down. Because she still didn't know what to do.

Then she laughed out loud. She didn't have to know what to do! There was someone else who would. Running to the phone, she lifted it and began dialing. Oh, yes, *she* would know. . . .

Rick smiled as a pair of dainty angels in long yellow gowns with ruffles at the shoulders and ankles came skipping out toward his car. His eyes flickered over the windows of the house, searching for a face that never appeared, or even the shadow of it, anything to tell him that she was in there, maybe sneaking a look out at him. Nothing. There was nothing. He sighed.

"Ladies," he said, alighting to open the car door with a flourish for the girls, "you are a delight to the eye and"—he sniffed appreciatively—"a treat for the nose. Did your mother say you could wear her best perfume?" Her best, and as far as he knew, her only. He'd bought it for her.

Jenny giggled as she slid over to sit by Roger. Pam smiled as she sat demurely, the perfect lady as always. "Yes, Rick. She put it on us herself."

"She's home?" So why hadn't she come to the door to see them off? He got behind the wheel. "What's she going to do this afternoon?"

"Rest."

"Rest?" he asked sharply. Sandy never rested! "Is she sick?"

"No, she's fine. Just tired. You know."

But that was just it. He didn't know. The kids had been strangely reticent about her the past week or so. He eyed Jenny narrowly in the mirror, but her face gave nothing away. Nor did Pam's.

"Rick? Shouldn't we leave? We don't want to be late."

With another look at the unadorned windows and closed door of the house, Rick put the car in gear and drove off.

As the music played, swelling and pulsing, he barely heard it, concentrating on the perfume of the children flanking him, breathing in Sandy's scent with every breath, worrying about her as usual. No, more than usual.

Why was she resting on a Sunday afternoon? Was she going out later? And with whom? Did he even have the right, anymore, to ask? No. No, he didn't. He had rejected her. He had let his hurt feelings get in the way of his good sense. He loved

her and she had said she wanted to marry him
and instead of leaping that damned ten-foot fence
again and running to her, he had told her she
would have to solve all her problems by herself,
deal with her insecurities on her own. What kind
of love refused to take the bad along with the
good? And if she hadn't called him after that
night, he had only himself to blame.

He must have injured her feelings, damaged her
pride as much as she had bruised his. Having
offered herself to him once, she would never do it
again and risk the kind of rejection her last offer
had been met with.

And what about him? It wasn't pride holding
him away from her now, it was fear. He was such
a coward. Yet, it was either go to her or lose her.
At least this way, not knowing for sure if she'd
listen to him, he had hope. But if he went to her
and she turned him away then he'd have nothing. . . .

He was glad when the last bars of *Peter and the
Wolf* were over and they could leave, and glad
when Pammy, with unexpected boldness, asked if
she could sit in the front seat. He wanted the
scent of her mother's perfume close to him. He
was doubly glad when, halfway home, she looked
at him and cried out, "Stop! Stop the car!"

He was at the curb, out his door, and hauling
her bodily out before he realized that she was not
about to throw up all over his upholstery. He
stared at her face. She didn't look sick. She looked

. . . ethereal, and she was gazing rapturously across the street as he set her down onto the sidewalk.

"Isn't it beautiful?" she said. "That's why I wanted to stop." Her blue eyes glowed up into his. "Please? Can we go in?"

"Into that church? But, Pam . . ." Dammit, he wanted to get home! He was tired of being a coward, and if Sandy was resting up for a hot date tonight, then he was determined to step in and stop it no matter what it took. She was his, and she was not going out with any other man!

"Please?" said Pam again. "I'd like to . . . pray," she added, looking nunlike.

Jenny, holding Roger's hand, had alighted from the backseat. Rick shot her an inquiring look.

"I'd like to go in too," she said. "We go to church with Granny and Granddad every Sunday when we're staying with them."

"Well, all right, go ahead. But try not to take too long, okay?"

"Let's all go," Jenny said. Taking Pam's hand, she led the way, leaving Roger to Rick. He followed them across the street, up the wide stone steps to the front doors, reached over them to open the latch, and then trailed inside after them.

The rousing strains of *Ode to Joy* swelled forth, filling the church, and Rick came to an abrupt halt as the girls, in procession, went slowly forward.

There was the scent of lemon oil, of leather, of ancient books and of flowers. Sun streamed at an

LIGHT ANOTHER CANDLE • 179

angle through a stained glass window, purpling the white hair of an occupant of a pew. The church was hushed and dim and the only other light came from the single, long slender candle held in the hand of the woman who stood on the right side of the altar, gazing at him over the steady flame. In her eyes shone total confidence, complete trust, absolute faith. . . .

And the light of a thousand candles.

Rick gazed back, rooted where he stood.

He felt weak. He was enormously strong. He felt choked. He was lightheaded with a sudden surge of oxygen. He felt a joyous laugh bubble up in his throat even as a massive sob shook his frame.

"Come on, Daddy," said Roger, sounding incredibly like Pam. "It'll be all right. I'll hold your hand."

He nearly left his son behind. He almost tripped over the slow-pacing girls, but his long legs would not—could not—slow their stride once they had started moving. He was hardly aware of the robed minister standing facing him, book open in hands, face composed as if the groom were the one to come walking in to his waiting bride every day.

His waiting bride . . . She was still watching him, just a hint of a smile on her lips. But how her eyes glowed as he took his place on her left.

She had tried to replicate the wedding gown he had bought her, but this one had cleaner, straighter lines and was perfect on her small, elegant frame.

She was as elegant as the tall figure who stood beside her, the person who could only, considering the position of this backward wedding party, be her "best woman", wearing a royal blue tuxedo-cut suit, her long white-shot hair piled high. Over Sandy's head Rick gave his mother an incredulous smile.

The minister cleared his throat.

The bride passed the candle to the groom, who took it in a sure and steady hand, looking into her eyes and seeing there the kind of everlasting glow he had known was within her. He turned and passed the candle to his—boy of honor?—and returned the beaming smile bestowed upon him. He caught the eyes of his two bridesmaids—grooms-maids?—in gold.

Pamela lowered her lashes demurely.

Jennifer, brimming over with silent glee, winked.

Rick turned back to Sandy, and her eyes still shone with those eternal flames. He took her hand as the minister instructed, but for him the ceremony was already complete. All had been said, all promises given, all vows made, in that simple passing from hand to hand of that flickering candleflame.

THE EDITOR'S CORNER

With the very special holiday for romance lovers on the horizon, we're giving you a bouquet of half a dozen long-stemmed LOVESWEPTs next month. And we hope you'll think each of these "roses" is a perfect one of its kind.

We start with the romance of a pure white rose, **IT TAKES A THIEF**, LOVESWEPT #312, by Kay Hooper. As dreamily romantic as the old South in antebellum days, yet with all the panache of a modern-day romantic adventure film, Kay's love story is a delight . . . and yet another in her series that we've informally dubbed "Hagen Strikes Again!" Hero Dane Prescott is as enigmatic as he is handsome. A professional gambler, he would be perfectly at home on a riverboat plying the Mississippi a hundred years ago. But he is very much a man of today. And he has a vital secret . . . one he has shouldered for over a decade. Heroine Jennifer Chantry is a woman with a cause—to regain her family home, Belle Retour, lost by her father in a poker game. When these two meet, even the sultry southern air sizzles. You'll get reacquainted, too, in this story with some of the characters you've met before who revolve around that paunchy devil, Hagen—and you'll learn an intriguing thing or two about him. This fabulous story will also be published in hardcover, so be sure to ask your bookseller to reserve a collector's copy for you.

With the haunting sweetness and excitement of a blush-pink rose, **MS. FORTUNE'S MAN**, LOVESWEPT #313, by Barbara Boswell sweeps you into an emotion-packed universe. Nicole Fortune bounds into world-famous photographer Drake Austin's office and demands money for the support of his child. Drake is a rich and virile heartbreaker who is immediately stopped in his tracks by the breathtaking beauty and warmth of Nicole. The baby isn't his—and soon Nicole knows it—but he's not about to let the girl of his dreams get out of sight. That means he has

(continued)

to get involved with Nicole's eccentric family. Then the fun and the passion really begin. We think you'll find this romance a true charmer.

As dramatic as the symbol of passion, the red-red rose, **WILD HONEY**, LOVESWEPT #314, by Suzanne Forster will leave you breathless. Marc Renaud, a talented, dark, brooding film director, proves utterly irresistible to Sasha McCleod. And she proves equally irresistible to Marc, who knows he shouldn't let himself touch her. But they cannot deny what's between them, and, together, they create a fire storm of passion. Marc harbors a secret anguish; Sasha senses it, and it sears her soul, for she knows it prevents them from fully realizing their love for each other. With this romance of fierce, primitive, yet often tender emotion, we welcome Suzanne as a LOVESWEPT author and look forward to many more of her thrilling stories.

Vivid pink is the color of the rose Tami Hoag gives us in **MISMATCH**, LOVESWEPT #315. When volatile Bronwynn Prescott Pierson leaves her disloyal groom at the altar, she heads straight for Vermont and the dilapidated Victorian house that had meant a loving home to her in her childhood. The neighbor who finds her in distress just happens to be the most devastatingly handsome hunk of the decade, Wade Grayson. He's determined to protect her; she's determined to free him from his preoccupation with working night and day. Together they are enchanting . . . then her "ex" shows up, followed by a pack of news hounds, and all heck breaks loose. As always, Tami gives us a whimsical, memorable romance full of humor and stormy passion.

Sparkling like a dew-covered yellow rose, **DIAMOND IN THE ROUGH**, LOVESWEPT #316, is full of the romantic comedy typical of Doris Parmett's stories. When Detective Dan Murdoch pushes his way into Millie Gordon's car and claims she's crashed his stakeout, she knows she's in trouble with the law . . . or, rather, the

(continued)

lawman! Dan's just too virile, too attractive for his own good. When she's finally ready to admit that it's love she feels, Dan gets last-minute cold feet. Yet Millie insists he's a true hero and writes a book about him to prove it. In a surprising and thrilling climax, the lady gets her man . . . and you won't soon forget how she does it.

As delicate and exquisite as the quaint Talisman rose is Joan Elliott Pickart's contribution to your Valentine's Day reading pleasure. **RIDDLES AND RHYMES,** LOVE-SWEPT #317, gives us the return of wonderful Finn O'Casey and gives him a love story fit for his daring family. Finn discovers Liberty Shaw in the stacks of his favorite old bookstore . . . and he loses his heart in an instant. She is his potent fantasy come to life, and he can't believe his luck in finding her in one of his special haunts. But he is shocked to learn that the outrageous and loveable older woman who owned the bookstore has died, that Liberty is her niece, and that there is a mystery that puts his new lady in danger. In midsummer nights of sheer ecstasy Liberty and Finn find love . . . and danger. A rich and funny and exciting love story from Joan.

Have a wonderful holiday with your LOVESWEPT bouquet.

And do remember to drop us a line. We always enjoy hearing from you.

With every good wish,

Carolyn Nichols

Carolyn Nichols
Editor
LOVESWEPT
Bantam Books
666 Fifth Avenue
New York, NY 10103

THE DELANEY DYNASTY

Men and women whose loves and passions are so glorious it takes many great romance novels by three bestselling authors to tell their tempestuous stories.

THE SHAMROCK TRINITY